RACE FOR SURVIVAL

Behind him, Cleve heard a packhorse scream, a dreadful cry that sent chills up his back. The maddened animal broke the halter and bolted past him through the snowfield, head flung back, eyes rolling, an arrow stuck shallowly in its haunch.

Cleve kicked his moccasined heels into his horse's flanks and tore after his wife's mare, Shadow, and the fleeing gelding, holding on to the lead rope. He hoped that no more of his string would be lost. The wind whipped his fur hood back from his ears, and the sounds of cries from those pursuing them came too clearly for comfort.

His wife, Second Son, was moving toward the concealment of the trees some half-mile down the eastern incline. His heart in his throat, Cleve raced after her, hearing shrill cries behind the deadly whisper of arrows flying past him.

WILDERNESS RENDEZVOUS

MOUNTAIN MAJESTY

Mountain Majesty

BOOK THREE

WILDERNESS RENDEZVOUS

JOHN KILLDEER

BANTAM BOOKS

NEW YORK · TORONTO · LONDON · SYDNEY · AUCKLAND

WILDERNESS RENDEZVOUS

A Bantam Domain Book / December 1992

ISBN 0-553-28887-3

Published simultaneously in the United States and Canada

Bantam Books are published by Bantam Books, a division of Bantam
Doubleday Dell Publishing Group, Inc. Its trademark, consisting
of the words "Bantam Books" and the portrayal of a rooster, is
Registered in U.S. Patent and Trademark Office and in other coun-
tries. Marca Registrada. Bantam Books, 666 Fifth Avenue, New York,
New York 10103.

PRINTED IN THE UNITED STATES OF AMERICA

RAD   0 9 8 7 6 5 4 3 2 1

chapter

— 1 —

The timber wolf was lank with winter, his ribs straining at his hide, his eyes sick and rheumy. Starvation stalked his heels, and he had hunted in vain for a rabbit or a chipmunk that had ventured out to search for an early sprig of grass.

When he scrabbled down the edge of the waterfall into the narrow valley, he was wavering on his legs, but a sound in the distance sent a surge of adrenaline through him. Ears pricking up, he turned toward the source of that thin wail. Some infant animal was there, and in his present condition that was all he was able to handle.

His teeth gleamed in the pale light, his tongue lolling from the corner of his muzzle. With dogged determination he set out for the source of the cry, even though the tang of smoke told him that a predator more dangerous than he might be very close by.

The wind sweeping down the narrow valley was chilled with snow, yet it held a faint scent that was a promise of spring as well. Cleve Bennett, stepping out of the tipi he shared with his wife and son, gazed through the stinging flakes and the dim dawn light, seeking some break in the clouds. Here in the mountain heights it seemed like winter, but he knew that down in the lower country spring had lit the valleys with blossom and greened them with grass.

The tribes—Absaroka, Kiowa, Shoshonni, Blackfoot—would be hunting, raiding for horses, stirring their winter-sluggish blood to action. It was going to be an interesting spring, for at present his family had as many plews as their horses could carry, and it was time to leave the safety of their valley to market them. That was going to be dangerous business.

He was thinking about the information he had obtained from Jules Terrebonne, trapper and fur thief. Cleve's former employer in the Rocky Mountain Fur Company, William Ashworth, was arranging to bring trappers and traders together at a rendezvous in early summer, where the harvest of the past winter's trapping could be sold or traded. This would save Cleve and Second Son the long journey back east to sell their furs, or the trek to the trading fort, where they were almost certain to be cheated.

It was to begin in June, and Cleve rummaged through his memory, trying to find what date this might be in the calendar he had left behind some years ago when he left Missouri. His first winter was spent on the Missouri River, forted up while Ashworth returned to St. Louis to replace the horses that had been stolen by Indians. The trappers had left there when the river thawed. Had that been April? Or was it in late March?

As he recalled each of the incidents sticking in his memory over the past seasons, he made another mark. With those as indicators he should be able to be accurate as to the year, if not the actual month.

He counted his marks. It had to be 1825. If they had arrived here by August, there had been . . . one . . . two . . . three . . . he counted moons, and then he realized that there were weeks and weeks when they had seen no glimpse of sky.

Second Son was no help, for the Cheyenne used a different system for keeping track of seasons. Even her monthly periods were of no use, for she'd been pregnant all that time.

He spat into a patch of snow, now dirty and bedraggled, and drew a deep breath. The fragrance of pine and spruce, the faint sulfur tang from the hot springs, the clean scent driving down the wind from the west filled him with a sense of well-being.

It had to be at least late April, though they still had storms that brought heavy snow to the surrounding peaks and ridges, falling mostly as rain in their almost inaccessible valley. Occasional snowslides off the steep cliffs reminded them how lucky they were to be sheltered in this spot. Even the occasional scouting Crow or Blackfoot had not troubled them in their winter quarters.

His dog, Snip, sniffed at his ankle, wagged his tail hopefully, and stared toward a patch of firs. He almost whined, though Snip seldom made a noise at all.

Cleve heard a faint gurgle from the thicket, but he deliberately didn't look in that direction. Cheyenne

ways of raising a baby were so different from any he had
ever known that they made him fiercely uncomfortable.

"Babies are supposed to cry!" he'd yelled at Second
Son the first time, while she bundled their week-old son
onto his cradleboard and started for the door flap.

She turned her dark eyes on him with an expression of
scorn. "You would risk your family, your furs, and your
life to allow a baby to cry? This is not acceptable. He will
learn, as I did and all my kind, not to make any noise.

"Yellow Hair, this is the way of my people, necessary
for survival. I will not die because my son is undisci-
plined, and neither will you." She glanced down at the
fur-wrapped bundle in her arms. "And neither will he."

She had stalked out, carrying the baby, board and all,
and he had followed to see what she was going to do. She
didn't spank the child or scold him. Instead, she took
him some distance from the tipi, checked the area for
any possible danger, and hung the board by its thongs
high in a tree on the downwind side.

Young Billy Wolf began howling lustily, but his mother
turned her back and returned to the tipi, shooing her
doubtful man before her. The cries behind them rose in
volume as the two moved out of eyeshot and into the tipi.
Cleve felt as if he were abandoning his child to the
elements.

"For Chrissakes, woman, that baby will go crazy, left
out there to himself. You cuddle a baby that cries. That's
the way my ma did me and my brothers. Or Pa whopped
us." He sat on a pile of furs and stuffed his fingers into
his ears so he couldn't hear the faint wails.

Second Son sat beside him and jerked his hands down
so he could hear her. "There is work to do. We must
make new moccasins before we go to this trading coun-
cil. We do not want to be shamed before all those other

white men because we are shabby. Here, set your foot on this."

She stretched a layer of dressed deerhide on the floor and touched his knee. Sighing, Cleve moved his foot, and she pushed off his scarred moccasin and set the foot firmly on the leather. With swift ease she traced the outline with charcoal from the fire, pushed the foot aside, and sliced out the strange shape of a Cheyenne moccasin.

Cleve found that watching her distracted him enough from the cries of his son that they didn't trouble him quite so much. He obediently changed feet and watched Second Son cut out the other moccasin.

Then she handed him the leather and several thongs and gestured for him to punch holes and lace the shoes together while she created her own.

"Hey! Listen!" He cocked his head, straining to hear. There was no sound but the soft sighing of the snow-laden wind around the smokehole. "Something's got him!"

She reached to lay her callused hand over his lips. "Yellow Hair, Cheyenne men do not make such a fuss over their young. Indeed, it is the part of their mother's brother to teach them and tease them and watch over them. My own brother, Singing Wolf, should rightfully be the one to do that, but as it is, we are too far, and our situation is . . . strange." She smiled mischievously, and he laughed.

"That's right. If you want to get technical, *I'm* his mother, because you are a warrior, and my brothers are way back in Missouri. But is he all right?"

"Of course." She looped a thong expertly through the holes she had punched in her first moccasin and gathered the leather into the correct shape, arranging the laps to fold around the ankle. "No one came, he got no attention, and so he stopped. Why cry when it gains you nothing and wears you out?''

Cleve thought about that as he painstakingly formed his own footgear. Once you considered it, the system made sense. Children yelled to get what they wanted. If they got nothing by it, they'd stop. He wondered why his own kind hadn't come up with such a simple solution.

Second Son had raced through the construction of her moccasins before the fire needed new fuel, and now she rose to her feet. "As he has stopped, then he will return to his family as a reward," she said.

There was a strained look about her eyes, and Cleve realized that she had been as anxious as he while their child was alone in the thicket. He reached to give her a hug around the hips.

"You're not fooling me," he said. "You want to run out and get him back as much as I do. So go. I'll work on my moccasins while you get him."

She was gone in a rush of displaced air, leaving him smiling down at his work. Almost before he missed her, she returned, her face flushed from the chill, the child clasped tightly to her chest.

Now, standing in the wind, listening for further sounds from the thicket, he remembered his vast relief when he saw that Billy Wolf had survived his first disciplinary exile.

This was the third. Second Son told him that probably after this the child would remember that his wails earned him nothing but loneliness. Cleve devoutly hoped so, for these times wore on his nerves.

A rushing, hissing crash echoed across the narrow valley. A mass of snow had slipped, he knew, burying the young pines and firs below the western cliffs under yards of chill white.

Until the compacted overhangs had fallen, it would not be safe to try hauling their furs up the sheer walls to the east. The horses would be unable to negotiate the perilous climb Cleve had managed to chip into the rock to allow them to get out of this valley, into which they had come with such difficulty.

Snip gave a shiver against his leg and looked toward the thicket again, his ears flicked forward, his tail still. He disapproved of Second Son's baby-training methods even more than his master did, for he adored young Bill. Now he stiffened and growled deep in his throat before shooting toward the fir trees like a black-and-white arrow.

The wolf slipped through a clump of small fir trees, his nose picking up the scent of tender young flesh. It was at some distance from the smoke, but if it had been nearby, he would not have hesitated. He must have food. His strength was fading, and if he sank into the snow of the valley's floor, he would, he knew, never rise from it again.

There was a lump hanging from a stub of a branch some distance up a tree. An easy leap when he was young and filled with red meat, but a hard one now. The wolf gauged the height, gathered his energies, and sprang as high as he could.

His teeth ripped through fur, and the infant screamed with fear. Before the timber wolf could leap again, something black and white shot through the needled branches of the young growth and bowled him over in a drift. Sharp teeth dug into his neck, and he felt his strength oozing away with the blood seeping from those wounds.

Steps crunched in the snow. The dying wolf looked up and saw a big shape, tall against the trees. Then something stabbed into his heart, and he died, his belly still empty, his hunger unsatisfied.

• • •

Cleve drew his knife from the skinny creature's heart and pulled Snip away from the ragged, strong-smelling body. He turned to the tree and felt over the bundle that was his son, who was still whimpering softly. He did not scream again, which told his father that the baby had learned his lesson about crying.

He patted the soft cheek and said, "You're all right, little one. You're all right," before turning to pull Snip from the pungent body of the wolf.

He felt him over, but except for a slash on the top of his head the dog was unhurt, though his heart was racing beneath his master's hands and his neck hair still bristled. Once Cleve set him down, he moved over beneath the still-hanging infant and looked up, whining softly.

A step sounded behind Cleve, and he turned to see Second Son coming through the thicket, headed toward the tree where the baby was hung. She stopped when she saw the dead wolf, and her face went very still. She said nothing, however, as she moved lithely past her husband and checked on their son.

She took the child from the tree and hung the thong around her shoulders. Billy Wolf hiccuped quietly but made no sound, and Cleve felt with gratitude that he was going to be all right now. No more exile into the tree! Now he would be safely in the tipi, where he belonged.

Thinking about the long journey through country where hostile people roamed, to the fork Terrebonne had spoken of, down on the Green River, Cleve knew that it would be far safer for them all because his son had been taught the Cheyenne way. Wild rivers and rough mountains lay between their home and the rendezvous. Wilder people, both red and white, inhabited those reaches, and by now Cleve was hardened to the knowledge that they would kill him or Second Son or the infant as quickly as they would anything else, game or man. Life was cheap, here in the Shining Mountains.

Another slithering crash resounded through the cold air. Let the fresh snow fall as it would, the earth was warming, and the foundations of the thick layers above were softening with spring. In a few weeks now he and his family would climb out and begin the long trek down from the Absarokas that would lead across the backbone of these mountains and down into the lower country along the Green.

He turned, sighing, into the tipi, where the coals glowed red and Second Son waited, nursing their son and watching meat roast over the fire. This was a lazy, contented life, once the trapping was done, but he was more than ready for a change.

The smell of the air made him restless, and a feeling of anticipation rippled through his nerves. Soon they would go. He was much more than ready.

His old teacher among those in the Ashworth group had told him about occasional random meetings among trappers. There was drinking, carousing, fighting. . . . Cleve felt his heart beat faster at the thought of trying his strength against that of others who were tough enough to live here in the mountains.

He'd tried to drink once, when one of the neighbors brought Pa a jug of applejack. He hadn't had time to drink anything but a sip, which tasted awful, but he still remembered the beating Pa had given him for stealing his liquor. He had a hankering to try again, this time with nobody to punish him for it.

He glanced over at Second Son. As if reading his thoughts, she smiled, her dark eyes sparkling in the red light of the fire. He wondered what she would make of the goings-on when numbers of whites got together.

Cleve yawned and stretched. Being a man, he was finding, was a lot better than being somebody's boy. He was ready to meet other men and trade blows and furs and lies. The sooner the better.

Billy Wolf gave a quiet gurgle, and Snip jerked and twitched in his sleep. Until then, Cleve thought, stretching, this was the best of lives.

chapter

— 2 —

Lifelong habit pulled at Second Son, making her long to change her campsite when the weather warmed, the snow melted, and small birds began singing their spring songs. Now their deep valley, a shelter when the blizzards blew, became a trap, its walls seeming to lean inward, ready to fall on her as she did the things necessary before they could take the trail out.

Shadow, her mare, felt the compulsion of the season's change as well. She had grown heavy with foal again in the long months since leaving Singing Wolf's village, and now she was very near to her time.

Second Son watched her carefully, for they could not risk her on the terrible climb out of the valley until she delivered her colt. The footing was precarious and the ramp Cleve had chipped was narrow. Her distended belly would make her too wide for the trail.

The young stallion that Second Son had stolen from the Pawnee in years past could make it without trouble, as could Socks, Cleve's gelding, and the horses they had taken from Henri Lavallette's winter camp. But the heavy mare was stuck until her load lightened.

Second Son's own offspring was growing by the day. Young Billy Wolf was not fat, but he was becoming longer, stronger, and more alert, his dark eyes snapping toward every sound, his hands reaching, his feet kicking as if trying to walk. He objected to his cradleboard more than any child she had seen; she could only suppose it was his father's blood that made him so impatient with confinement.

Yet he had learned his lesson well. He made no sound, except when she set him on her knee and talked to him, both in the English she had learned from Cleve and her friend Holy William, for whom he had been named, and in her own tongue, which she was determined he would understand. When he met her brother, Singing Wolf, she wanted him to be able to talk with his uncle. The two of them were destined to be companions, she felt, for Wolf Sings on the Mountain—Billy Wolf's full Cheyenne name—was a kindred name and totem to that of Singing Wolf.

She was carrying her son on her back, tied firmly into his board, when she went to check on Shadow. It was now spring, even in the high country, and the streams ran loudly with snowmelt, the green plants were already knee-high, and the overhangs of snowpack had fallen and disappeared among the rocks lining the cliffs.

The mare was standing, head down, in her favorite patch of grass. Her gaze was thoughtful when it met that of Second Son, and when she put out her nose and snuffled at the warrior's hand, it was absentmindedly, as if she listened to something inside herself.

Second Son recognized the signs, for it had not been long since she had done the same, waiting for her son to come to birth. That had been a day etched in her memory, for it had also brought an end to her old enemy Jules Terrebonne. The thought of leaving him bound to a tree, waiting for the cold or a grizzly to make an end to him, was a deep satisfaction to her.

She stroked the mare's ears, scratched under her chin, and clucked softly. An inquiring gurgle from behind made her smile and turn so the child could also look into the horse's eyes.

Already the boy was fascinated by their animals, and it proved that his Cheyenne heritage was strong. Her people were natural horsemen, and he showed signs of following in their ways. That was a necessity in the world of the plains and mountains, and she felt certain that he would surpass his father in riding skills.

Cleve, whatever his other virtues, did not become a part of Socks when he rode, though the horse was trained to do things that it never would have occurred to any of her kind to teach a mount.

The mare gave a long sigh, followed by a groan of effort. The warrior woman laid her hand on her neck and closed her eyes. Shadow was growing old, and Second Son had noticed all her life that older animals tended to have more difficulty with birth. This would not be the first time her mare had such trouble.

But it was early yet. The colt was a long way from being born. She turned at last and went to the tipi, where she found Cleve cleaning mud off his outer moccasins and cursing softly as Snip warmed himself by the fire.

"Yellow Hair, why do you sing that song?" she asked.

She hung the cradleboard from its post, which was fixed into the ground, and turned her attention to the venison hanging above the blaze on a tall tripod.

After giving the meat a twirl, which scattered droplets of fragrant steam into the coals, she began rolling the furs that had made their bed for so long. It was getting to be too warm for buffalo robes and beaver blankets.

"This damn mud is sticky as glue. I don't know how we're going to move once we get out of here, if we ever do. The horses may mire up to their bellies, if the top of the ridge is like the bottom of the valley."

That was the sort of silly statement she had learned was peculiar to white men. "The ridge is drained well, for the water came down here. When we get up there, the ground will be covered with damp fir and spruce needles, anyway.

"Why do you fret? We will go when we can go and not before. Be patient and play with your son, if you have nothing better to do."

This was a sharper statement than she usually offered, no matter how irritable she became, and he glanced up, concerned. "Shadow?" he asked, knowing that some private worry would explain the tartness of her tone.

She nodded as she tied the thongs holding their blankets rolled together. "She is getting old, Yellow Hair. She has been my friend since I had only twelve summers, and if she should die, it would make me sad. She seems all right, but I have seen old mares die, unable to push the colt out."

"There are things to do for that," he said. "Don't you remember how I helped her when I was a guest of the Burning Hearts?"

Second Son suddenly recalled to mind that long-ago scene, almost forgotten in the difficulties and dangers of their lives since that time. He had, indeed, saved her mount by reaching in and easing the colt through without breaking its legs or its neck. White men, for all their strange ways, had skills that were valuable.

"I forgot." She smiled. "That makes me feel much happier. Will you go with me to see how she is doing?"

"The venison is almost ready. I have a space in my belly that you could put that mare into. After we eat, I'll see what can be done." He wiped his hands on his buckskin breeches and reached for the meat knife.

They left Snip to watch the baby when they returned to the grass patch to check on Shadow. If this was like the situation they had faced before, it would take both to bring the colt. Second Son dreaded that, but as they neared the mare's retreat they heard a soft whicker, followed by a thin bleat of sound.

She had done it alone! Cleve reached for Second Son's hand and they ran together to see the newcomer.

Still dark with wet, the little creature turned to face them, its head down, its sides heaving. Then it reversed itself and began nuzzling beneath the mare, looking for her teat. Shadow gazed smugly at them over the spindly-legged foal, and her sigh was one of great relief and satisfaction.

Second Son reached to touch her nose, not getting too near. Then she turned to Cleve. "In three days we can go. She will gain strength now, and we already have the furs ready to haul up the cliff. You can take the horses up one by one and have them ready when we get the last of the bales on the ridge.

"I have become restless here. It is good to move, Yellow Hair. I cannot think how your people bear to live in houses rooted to the land."

"What are you going to call the little 'un?" he asked her. He was stroking the damp curls of hair along the colt's back, feeling the bony structure of his ribs and

spine and the shape of his barrel, as well as the confor-
mation of his legs.

She walked around to look at the head, which emerged
between its mother's legs from time to time as it butted
too hard and lost the teat. A jagged streak of white
marked the face from nose to forelock.

"Blaze will do well," she said. "And he will belong to
our son. Bill and Blaze—in English those go together
well, do they not?"

He grinned at her, and she felt once again the surge of
warmth that this pale-eyed husband of hers so often gave
her. He was not like the Tsistsistas in many ways. He had
a gentleness that the men of her tribe seldom allowed to
show. But he had a sense of humor that they appreciated
a great deal. It was no mistake when she captured him
for her "wife," back on the Belle Fourche.

It took three days of constant effort to take the bales of
plews up the cliff from their high cave. Cleve climbed to
the top, taking the animals up one by one and securing
them on a picket line. Then he let down the rawhide
ropes.

Second Son, who had the surest of feet, clambered
about the cavern high in the cliff, which had sheltered
their furs from the damp of winter. She tied the line
around each bale, pushing it over the lip of the cave to
swing free, and then leaned out perilously to give it a
boost upward.

Cleve harnessed Socks's strength in raising the heavy
bales. They had spent days making the strong rawhide
lines, and a pair of them was passed around a smoothed
log, forming a pulley. Socks moved on command, walking away and drawing the line smoothly over the wooden
roller, until he reached a point at which Cleve could

reach the bale and swing it onto the clifftop, once it cleared the edge.

Used to farm work back in Missouri, the gelding didn't object to his task, though the other horses protested when Cleve tried them at it. Every day saw more of the bales in place, protected from the weather by dressed deerhides and the batwing shape of buffalo hide that had formed the walls of their tipi.

Snip prowled below, staring up at his master and Second Son, whimpering softly from time to time and keeping an eye on Bill, who was, as usual, hung high in a tree, faced so he could see his parents at work. Second Son knew that no danger could approach the child without the dog's giving warning, so she worked, unworried, until all the plews were secured.

Now it was time to leave this hidden valley. She had seen it first when she was very young, newly admitted as a warrior to the band. Her brother had stood up there on that cliff, pointing downward and saying that this was a good place to remember.

"If you are ever pursued by enemies too numerous to fight alone, remember this place. It may serve you well as a refuge." The words were addressed to Red Fox, who was the leader of their group of youngsters, but she had never forgotten, and a refuge it had indeed proved.

Those enemies who had followed them the summer before had not ventured past the valley filled with smoke and bubbling mud. Or if they had, they had never thought to look into this forbidding place into which they would have to let themselves and their horses down with rawhide lines. From above it seemed uninhabited, she knew, for she and Yellow Hair made certain of that after setting up their tipi.

It had been a place that had seen much happiness and some sadness. She thought of their friend Holy William, now lying alone in the valley to the west, his grave guarded by the bones of Jules Terrebonne, which were probably scattered now by scavengers.

He had been a friend, however much she had distrusted him at first. She felt saddened that he hadn't lived to see his small namesake, for he had anticipated the child's birth with pleasure. Used to the terrible mortality that could overtake the very young, she had never seen a man who seemed so intensely interested in the arrival of a child.

But her people did not brood over death, no matter whether the lost one was young or old, for that distracted the mind and wasted energy. She turned again to descend into the valley and take her son down from the branch where he was hung. Snip wagged frantically around her legs as she signaled to Cleve, atop the cliff, that she was ready to begin the last climb. He dropped the rope to her, and she looped it about her and the cradleboard.

The rock was slick with wet as she set her moccasins carefully, balancing the cradleboard on her back as Cleve kept tension on the line from above.

Billy Wolf was quiet as they went up the face of the rock, using the old ascent rather than the one hacked out for the horses. She felt able to climb all day—to fly like the hawk already poised on a column of air, waiting for prey to appear below. The bird's scream echoed between the walls of the valley as she went up and gained the top.

They were going to travel through the mountains, to visit a place where she would meet others like Yellow Hair. Although she had been taught from birth to suppress her emotions, she felt a flutter of excitement deep inside.

There were weapons, Cleve told her, even finer than

those they had from Lavallette's store. There were metal implements useful as cookpots and knives, for which they could trade plews. Again the excitement welled up in her, but she suppressed it sternly and stepped out onto the top of the cliff.

Cleve waited, and together they loaded the bales onto the restless horses, who were snuffling and whinnying with this unexpected change in their routine. Then they turned their mounts to follow this ridge to the obscure path by which they had come.

They were alert; Snip ranged ahead, his nose in the air, sniffing for danger. This was their world, and it contained, Second Son knew all too well, a multitude of enemies.

chapter

— 3 —

It had been a rough couple of years. Though he had trapped and hunted and made war with one tribe or another in the mountains and the plains for well over a decade, Emile Prevot had seldom had such a difficult expedition as this one organized by his friend William Ashworth.

First, Ashworth's group had lost their horses when their journey was just begun, and that had cost them a full summer of travel toward their goal. The winter in the fort they had put up near the Missouri River was one of his less happy memories, for there had been no women— even red-skinned ones—no liquor after a few months, and much horseplay and quarreling.

Keeping those rambunctious young *Américains* occupied and out of mischief had been a hard task, and he felt worn-out just thinking about it. He kicked his horse into a jog and signaled to those behind him to keep close.

This was a route that those headed for the rendezvous at Henry's Fork on the Green River would be expected to take. He had known for years about the depredations of men who preferred ready-caught-and-cured furs to getting their own the hard way. He had no intention of running into another ambush like that back at the Arikara villages, where they had lost several men, a number of horses, and decided to abandon their keelboat and proceed across country on horseback.

Since that time the band of young trappers had scattered into the mountains, though some twenty had regrouped for this first great trading get-together. Behind him rode Jim Bridwell, older now and wiser than he had been as an eighteen-year-old fresh from a farm in Kentucky.

William Shooner was there, too, alone and looking grim. He had volunteered nothing, and Emile had not yet ventured to ask about his brother, Vince, who had gone with him so lightheartedly into the mountains to take the finest beaver ever trapped by man. Bill's bales were good ones, but his expression was not happy.

Paul Levreaux had trapped alone, as was his habit. He emerged from the upper ranges of the Bighorns in time to meet Emile at the agreed-upon spot, where they waited for the others to join them. He brought with him a few remnants of clothing and bone that in life had been one of his former companions. How he died was anyone's guess.

Emile was anxious to reach the security of the rendezvous so he could ask about everyone, but this was not the time or the place. They must ride, with their laden packhorses almost groaning beneath the weight of valuable plews, as if every ravine, every rock, every tree hid enemies with theft on their minds. Which, of course, they might well do.

Emile gestured for Bridwell to ride up, and they halted to speak before entering the long defile before them. Once into the ravine leading down to the river, they would be squeezed between those high walls, their only route forward or back. He had to know that they weren't walking into a trap.

"You go along the high groun', eh?" he said to the younger man. "If someone wait there for us, we like to know, *n'est-ce pas?*"

Bridwell grinned, but his smile no longer held the feckless joy it had in the past. This was a far grimmer man than the one Emile had sent into the mountains. His eyes held the memory of terrible things, and again Emile longed to hear the story of his winter alone.

But he waved him forward, and Bridwell dismounted and slipped into the ragged fringe of pines along the rim of the canyon. Bridwell was a fast runner, almost as fast as their lost Cleve Bennett. He would cover ground quickly and return soon.

While they waited, Emile slipped the bit of his mount and loosed the hackamores of pack animals so his horses could graze on the spring grass; the others followed suit. Levreaux kindled a fire, and soon coffee boiled in the soot-blackened pot and strips of jerky came out of packs to be shared. There was no point in wasting this respite, for Prevot wanted to reach Henry's Fork as soon as possible. Such a burden of valuable fur bales was best disposed of quickly.

He loved the wild country, yes. He would never voluntarily return to the slums of Paris, which had been his birthplace, or even to the mud of New Orleans, where he had once owned a share in a very busy brothel. But he was also a practical man who trapped for profit, and his take was a handsome one. Being one of Ashworth's lieutenants, he knew that the prices for the bales on the packhorses would be better than fair.

The young trappers brought west by Ashworth a couple of years before were paid by the year for their efforts, but Prevot, as a senior member and trainer of these wild youngsters, had been promised a share in Ashworth's profits. That should amount to a considerable sum.

The trading forts, Lisa's and shorter-lived ones, had a reputation for cheating the trappers, selling watered whiskey and inferior goods at greatly inflated prices. But Prevot, canny Parisian that he was, knew all the tricks, and what he brought away from the rendezvous would be worth the effort he put into his work. He would not be shortchanged. Unless, of course, he caught a case of the clap.

He chuckled aloud, and Levreaux glanced up at him, a quizzical smile on his narrow face. "You think of *les femmes*, Emile. I know the look. I, too, am not too old to think of them. And these *hommes* we bring with us, they will disappear, I think, into the tipis where the young squaws are and they will not come out until all their gold is gone."

"But we old men, we are too wise for that, *n'est-ce pas?*" Emile poured another dollop of inky coffee into his battered tin cup. "Though I recall the time, *mon ami*, when I have stagger away from the trade fort with only trap and horse, and owe the trader for the supply I take for another winter."

He drank off the scalding liquid. His taste buds had known so many vile and painful doses that this one was almost pleasant.

There was a low muttering from time to time as men caught up with the doings of the past winter, but frequently that came to a halt while all heads turned toward the canyon along whose rim Bridwell had gone on scout. The wind sang among the pines overhead, and the sounds of insects mingled with the distant skree of an eagle, but no shot or shout came to their ears.

Prevot had an almost animal sharpness of hearing. Paul Levreaux had always claimed that he could hear a blizzard blowing before it came over the horizon, a cougar prowling in the distance, the very grass growing. Now he directed that acute sense toward the canyon, and what he heard brought him upright from his crouch over the fire.

He dumped the contents of the coffeepot onto the coals, kicked dirt over everything, and gestured for his men to take cover. Footsteps pounded toward them, not audible as yet to anyone except him.

Bridwell would not be running unless he had bad news to tell. This was full-out flight, and even as he lay flat behind a slab supporting squarish boulders, Prevot began to sense the thuds of pursuing feet, as well.

Jim had stuck his nose into a nest of hornets, it seemed. All around him Emile heard ramrods pushing home loads, knives slipping out of sheaths, and hatchets being laid conveniently to hand.

These were now old hands, who had survived the long months alone. Of sixty men who had come from Missouri with the Ashworth group, Emile suspected that fewer than forty survived, if so many. These twenty had proven their ability to cope with sudden dangers and unexpected enemies, and he felt far more comfortable in their company than he ever had with any others. Greenhorns were dangerous companions, but these could no longer be called that.

Now others among the men pricked up their ears and looked toward the distant figure that bounded toward them, his rifle in hand, his red hair gleaming in the sunlight. Somewhere he had lost his badgerskin cap, Prevot noted, and his long locks fluttered on the wind.

Emile laid his rifle along the boulder and aimed past Bridwell, waiting for the first target to come into sight. But those who pursed the runner were cautious men; not until the young man vaulted over the outlying line of stones and dropped from sight did the first shadow flicker between two distant lodgepole pines.

There was no time for a shot, but Emile marked the position of that shadow before he turned his gaze back to the arrival of the next. Behind him he heard Bridwell crawling toward him, his breath coming short, his heart's quick beating practically audible.

"A couple dozen men . . . five miles down the river canyon. Lots of horses. Not . . . Indians. Horses . . . loaded with plews. Trappers. You think . . . they're pirates like those . . . you told us about . . . back at Fort Henry?" He plunked down beside Prevot and re-loaded his own rifle.

"There was one ver' bad man call Jules Terrebonne. He have band of other bad man. They steal fur from anyone, white skin or red. But now there may be more. I cannot tell until I see. Some in that cadre I know. Terrebonne I would recognize if it is five mile away." He narrowed his eyes, trying to make his vision match his hearing.

But there was no more movement on the track of their scout. That was suspicious, and Prevot turned to scan his line. "Levreaux, you take ten and go back behin' where the rock thin away. I think those man they try to flank us, *n'est-ce pas?*"

Paul nodded briefly. He, too, had survived long years

among the perils of this wide land, and he knew the strategies of all sorts of enemies as well as Emile did. He raised a finger, and Bill Shooner wriggled backward to join him. The men at the rear of the line did not wait, but moved to follow Levreaux beyond the intervening out-thrusts of stone.

No word had been spoken to warn any listener of the change of defense strategy. After Emile heard the first volley of shots from behind, he heard, on its heels, a leisurely series of replies from the flintlocks of his own people.

He had no time to listen to the cries of pain from those who had expected to surprise them, however, for another rain of rifle balls arrived against the stones shelter-ing him and his other men. He peered through the crevice between two boulders and saw a flickering of motion among the scrub at the edge of the small clear-ing edging the upthrust of rock. His Henry roared, filling the air with smoke, and he sank behind the slab and moved upwind to aim again, reloading as he went.

The shapes of men were almost hidden in the rising clouds of black powder smoke, but he aimed coolly and fired with deliberation, making certain that no one on this side of the outcrop came near the natural barrier. Beside him he heard Bridwell's musket firing, too.

After a time there was no target at which to shoot, and Emile set his ear to the rock to catch any step moving over the ground while the smoke obscured his vision. He could hear nothing; behind them the firing had stopped. Then he heard the thuds of horses moving away in the distance.

"They are leave now," he murmured to Bridwell. "I hear the hoof go away down the draw. Raise the hat, eh, James, to see if it is shoot." He took from his head his worn foxskin cap and handed it to the younger man.

Bridwell grinned, his face grimed with powder and dirt, and raised the bedraggled fur on the barrel of his musket.

A single shot whirled it around madly, the tail flying out at an angle. But that was the last, and no other sound was heard except the whisper of wind in pines.

A scraping of rock on rock told Emile that the rear echelon was moving toward him again, and he pushed himself up and peered over the rock. The wind had thinned the clouds of smoke to drifts that lay in flat layers, and no sign could be found there of anyone. High above them he heard the derisive scream of the eagle, as if the bird felt only contempt for the puny abilities of men to kill one another.

"We have send them away," he said to Paul, who now stood beside him. "But someplace between here and the fork we may find them wait once more, for they know we carry many fine fur. We must take care, *mon ami*. What do you think?"

Levreaux stared through the dwindling wisps of powder smoke at the dark blotch that was the farther wall of the canyon into which they had intended to ride. "I think we go another way, Prevot. They have descend into that place, and from old I know there is no way to depart from it with horse and bale. Only at either end can the horse find footing."

He shrugged his shoulders, his greasy leather shirt crinkling at the folds. His eyes were narrowed, the pale gray irises glinting between his eyelids as he gazed into a place Emile could not see.

This was an old habit of Paul's that impressed all who knew him. He could take the known and from it he could extrapolate possible future actions that often proved to be deadly accurate.

"We send half our band southward to that other pass

we know. They take the fur and the packhorse with them, so we do not have to worry with them. There should be little risk of meet those pirate on that route, *n'est-ce pas*? Even though it is much more difficult than this one.

"We take the rest and go the long way aroun', leaving many track. If they come back to see why we do not come, they will not know which to follow. We will meet . . . here." He knelt and drew a quick map in the dust, jabbing a dot into a point far to the south and west of their present location.

Prevot mulled over the suggestion, his slow, thorough mind looking for flaws. When he could find no major ones, he nodded. "We do that thing," he said.

Turning, he gestured for Bridwell and Shooner to come up and join the planning. "I send you two, with ten more to help if they should follow, and you meet us there, eh?" He stared from face to face. Both young men looked disappointed.

"You mean we got to go around them bastards down there without any fight?" asked Bridwell. He pushed his hair out of his eyes impatiently. "Lost my damn hat," he muttered.

"You will be entrust with all the fur, *mes amis*. We will rely on you to take them through safe to the fork, you understand? And there may be other men on that route who will also want them—or the hair upon your heads. The fight you may have, before you arrive!"

He moved to his pack, which he had left on his horse, and pulled out a droopy wool hat. "Here, you cover your head with this. Then the sun, she will not cook your brain, *n'est-ce pas*?"

Bridwell took the worn thing, which immediately flopped over his hand. But he donned it, pinning back the front part of the brim with a large thorn broken from a stickery bush. His long face looked strange beneath the chapeau, Emile thought, like an intelligent young horse's.

"Then go. We will stay here for some while, to see if they come to find us. If they do, then we will have the fight before you. If not, we will make all speed toward the meet with you. Now go, *mes amis*. We do not want anyone to know that you have all the plew, eh?"

But it was with some misgiving that he watched them out of sight, the horses snorting with irritation at having their rest interrupted. "They will go fast, those *jeunes hommes*," he said to Levreaux. "But we go smart, *n'est-ce pas?*"

chapter

— 4 —

The streams ran deep and swift with the thunderous waters plunging down from snowmelt as the small band of horses, led by Second Son and the infant, moved through the steep ways leading down from their hidden valley. Cleve felt some apprehension as he scouted the crossing into each of the succeeding glens, for it had been there that his party had found Crow when they moved through the mountains the summer before.

But the tribes seemed to have left on some business in other places, for, as they traveled, there was no hint of danger from any except an occasional grizzly sow, overly protective of her roly-poly cubs. Second Son assured him that such untroubled passage was not normal, and Cleve doubled his efforts to see and hear everything. He didn't intend to be caught napping just because things had been quiet so far.

When they came out on a high, bare ridge and Second Son pointed to the west, saying "Look, Yellow Hair. The Ghost Mountains!" he hardly turned.

But then, just visible above the intervening ridges and forests, he saw the tops of those silver-pale mountains for the first time, and his breath caught in his throat. Their heads thrust up through the cloud layer that lay over the sky; they seemed almost like living giants, brooding over the spaces below their hidden peaks.

He shivered as Second Son pointed again, this time southward toward a distant river, winking like pewter far below their present position. "We will follow that for a time," she said. "And then we will climb again. To find the river you seek will mean a long journey, and there are others in the mountains. We must take great care."

But the journey continued as if under some blessing, without interruption as they climbed and descended, struggled through steep ravines and out into lush valleys. They began finding the droppings of horses on trails they crossed, as well as prints of moccasins beside streams, and Cleve redoubled his vigilance.

They were moving up a deep creek, which was rushing headlong down its channel as it meandered from the heights above. This was a steeper way than the main route, but it was shorter, Second Son said, and it would cut days off their journey.

Cleve dismounted where the narrow track curved around an outcrop of rock that thrust out into the stream, creating an unceasing roar and a dash of spray.

From here on it was too steep for riding. They had to lead the horses carefully so that one did not dislodge some delicately balanced stone on the cramped ledge forming the path and go plunging to its death, carrying with it his scanty supplies.

Chipmunks skittered across the tops of the damp stones, their eyes bright and beady as they watched the intruders pass. Second Son ignored them, as well as the pine squirrels that were frisking in the overhanging trees, though Cleve watched them, when he could, chuckling at their antics.

Their course lay upward, and he moved steadily, slowing only when the ground was so soft or the rock so slick that it posed a danger. The terrain grew steeper all the while.

As they climbed, it grew colder. More snow encumbered the forest's floor, and the slant of the slope grew steeper. The air, tanged with pine below, changed to the fragrance of spruce and fir as they moved up to the tree line and passed beyond the last thin, warped outliers.

Snip, ranging outward regularly, began sniffing the air and coming back to look up into Cleve's eyes as if trying to convey some message to his master. At last he took up a position between Socks and the packhorses and remained there, though from time to time he would turn his nose toward their backtrail.

Second Son halted Shadow at the edge of a wide expanse of melting snow and turned, too, listening. Her hand came up, and Cleve went still, for her face was wearing its warrior look for the first time since they had disposed of Terrebonne.

Bare ridges lay about them, still layered beneath fields of white. Dark spines of stone loomed black against the snow, and the wind, cold and clean as a nun's conscience, knifed past Cleve's ears on its endless journey across those sterile heights, whining and whistling past his fur-clad skull.

The peak rising to his right was dark against the sky, its

gray mass of boulders shining with wet. Though Snip and Second Son ignored the cliff above them, Cleve studied the abrupt slope, trying to pick out any motion, any shape, any color that should not be there. Only the wind, lifting snow from hidden pockets and drifting it along its current, seemed to move.

Cleve knew that acute ears were checking even the slightest sound amid the wind and the hiss of blown snow. When his companion drew a quick breath, he knew she had heard something. Instantly she heeled Shadow into a lope, risking her delicate legs among the hidden stones. Cleve jerked the lead rope to bring the packhorses along behind Socks.

Snip, as if relieved, darted ahead and over the long rise of snow, to disappear beyond the crest. If any enemies lurked there, the dog would find them.

They were halfway along the slope when warriors broke from the trees behind them, their shrill whoops echoing from the cliff.

Cleve pounded after Second Son along the sloping expanse. To their right the height cut off any flight, and to the left the snowfield ended in an impossible descent. Only ahead, over the crest, was there the promise of escape, for he could see trees, dark against the sky, waiting there.

Snip appeared, a dark dot on white, and came swiftly to meet Second Son. He paused, his neck hair bristling as he saw the distant warriors. Then he turned and dashed back the way he had come. Cleve knew his dog all too well—Snip had found some refuge, there beyond the snow slope.

Behind him he heard a packhorse scream, a dreadful cry that sent chills up his back. The maddened animal broke the halter holding it to the line and bolted past him through the snowfield, head flung back, eyes rolling, an arrow stuck shallowly in its haunch.

Cleve kicked his moccasined heels into Socks's flanks and tore after Shadow and the fleeing gelding, holding on to the lead rope and hoping that no more of his string would be lost. The wind whipped his fur hood back from his ears, and the sounds of cries from those pursuing them came too clearly for comfort.

Second Son was moving down the far side of the clear area now, toward the concealment of the trees, which were some half mile down the eastern incline. His heart in his throat, Cleve raced after her, hearing shrill cries behind the whisper of arrows, which now began flying past him.

It could hardly have been five minutes from beginning to end, but that seemed the longest ride of his life. When he joined his wife in the screen of firs that rapidly grew thicker as they descended the slope, he felt as if he had been riding for his life for many days.

Except for the single packhorse, which now must be dashing madly down the mountainside, all their animals were still secure. The furs, which had to be what those behind wanted from them, were still in his hands.

Snip came out of the trees, watching his people race toward him for a moment, and disappeared again into the dark trunks of the spruces. His tracks were deeper dimples in the snow that was already pocked with drips from the snowmelt in the trees, but Second Son turned unerringly in the right direction and followed the tracks, knowing the dog enough now to trust his guidance.

Once they were well among the spruces and firs, the ground was bare of snow, only single patches on the shaded side of certain huge trunks still showing white against the duff of needles and bark that had fallen over the years.

Now their animals left little trace of their passing. When Snip led them to a tangled outcrop of rock that angled back into the slope of the mountain, Cleve knew this would mean the possibility of a more even fight.

A long spur that looked as if taffy candy had melted, run, and then hardened was the first of the barriers, and they rode around it and dismounted, pushing the horses into the cramped space between it and a jumble of broken rocks, weathered loose from the formation behind it.

Instantly, Cleve moved back along their trail to brush away the telltale tracks of their two mounts, which was not hard, for the ground here was covered with fir needles, centuries deep. He found the clear track of the packhorse farther along, churning up the snow and needles enough for any number of animals. Maybe the pursuers would follow that trail instead of turning aside.

Second Son, when he returned, had led all the horses except Socks far around to the end of the outcrop, securing them closely to spurs of stone so that nothing except an Indian wielding a knife could loose them. She had placed Billy Wolf, on his cradleboard, in a notch in the rock, where no random arrow could find him, and Snip stood guard beside the infant, his nose pointed defiantly toward their still-unseen enemies.

"I saw them," she said softly into his ear. "Pawnee. I know them for many years, and they are fierce warriors, anxious for the horses and women of other tribes. These furs, Yellow Hair, may be paid for with even more deaths before we are done. But this is a good day to die." She nodded decisively, and he saw in her eyes that fierce glint he had seen in those of her brother, Singing Wolf, back there on the plains with the Burning Heart Cheyenne.

"Maybe they'll follow the gelding. It stirred up the ground enough to misguide them."

She shook her head. "Never. The Pawnee, when they track, remain on the trail until they catch their prey. They have seen our loaded horses, probably from a lookout that we could not see as we moved. They will want them, and the beaver will only add to their lust. A Pawnee lives for coups, and this would be a great one."

Cleve posted himself behind an overgrown chunk of rock fallen from the spur. Above him the outcrop loomed, its upper part overhanging the area below as if it had hardened in the act of overflowing. Hidden well, he could see the track down which the first of his pursuers should come.

After a time he heard the light crunch of footsteps in the mulch of the forest as unmounted warriors darted from tree to tree down the incline, keeping a close watch about them, though they glanced at the ground only to be certain they still followed the hoof marks of the wounded horse.

Pawnee, of course, as Second Son had said. The scalp locks were plain against the sky beyond them, and their lack of paint told him they had not been on a raid. Their finding his party was one of those nasty accidents that seemed to be part of living in this wild country.

The soft-footed warriors passed like shadows among the trees, leaving hardly a track in the patches of snow as yet unmelted. When the last had disappeared downhill, he withdrew into the depths of the overhang with Second Son.

"They passed us. Looked like about fifteen, from what I could see. Maybe we ought to move while they're chasing that crazy horse." He waited for her answer, for she was the one who knew the Pawnee best.

"They will come back. But maybe we will be fortunate

again, Yellow Hair. I do not like waiting like this for enemies to find us. We will go." She turned at once to take Bill onto her back, and Cleve led Socks behind her to the other horses. In a few moments they were making their way as quietly as possible along the slope, heading for the ridge Second Son thought was beyond the forest to the west.

The layered needles, damp from the winter's snow, were slick underfoot, and Cleve had to watch his step to keep from slipping sideways down the abrupt incline. Cautiously he moved forward, keeping Socks on a close rein behind him, almost treading on his heels. He could only hope the pack animals, strung along after them, would make no misstep.

They had gone perhaps a mile, as quickly as they felt was possible, when there came a long cry behind them. It wasn't loud, but clearly it called to the Pawnee that the trail had been found once more.

Cleve looked at Second Son and then both stared about them. They were on a steep mountainside; the trees were thick but not thick enough to hide them. Behind was the outcrop, which was only a kind of trap. Ahead was a dark bulk showing through the spruces. It seemed, as they neared it, to be a rockslide that could give cover.

A long toe of black rock appeared, with fair-sized trees growing around it. Beyond was another wild tumble of debris, slanting up the mountain and crannied by wind and weather.

Behind those was a veritable maze of slides thrusting from the parent landslip along with boulders larger than houses, many of them at least the size of horses. It was an admirable spot for an ambush, if there was protection from those who might come down from above, risking the rotten stone as they descended.

Second Son secured the cradleboard to Socks's back and turned to stare upward. "I will go to the other end. If enemies come down from above, we are lost. We must know if it is possible. I will make sure of that. But I wonder about that up there. Can you climb to see if any might come down it?"

Cleve nodded. "I think so. If I can't go up, then it's pretty sure nobody can come down without jumping an awfully long way."

As she disappeared among the boulders he looked up at the dark breast of rock above him, trying to pick out possible hand- and foot-holds. He wanted no enemy at his back.

He managed to climb some twenty yards before he came to bare stone, revealed by the slip below it. It was smooth and slick, impossible to pass for something like fifty yards. Anyone trying that route would shoot down it as if on a slide and would end up at the foot of the mountain or wrapped around a tree below.

Reassured, he jumped down the last few feet and led Socks and his burden deep into shelter behind the rock bastions. Second Son returned, her face set. "They may come from that direction, but they must go a long way around. They might send a handful, with so many of them and only two of us. But perhaps we can deal with those behind before others can make that long trek and take us from the rear."

The two settled themselves strategically, Cleve lying flat behind the first rocks, aiming between boulders from a sheltered position. Second Son climbed up the second tumble and hid between two more, protected by solid rock on three sides and a shallow lump on the fourth.

Then they waited.

The first Pawnee came creeping on his belly toward

the rocks from the tree shadows beyond. Cleve watched him approach until he was near enough for a certain shot with his flintlock. Then he took aim and blew the top of the warrior's head away.

That made those who followed cautious, and they fanned out, uphill and down. It made Cleve nervous to think of one of the painted devils climbing up toward his family from downslope while he concentrated on those directly ahead of him, but there was nothing to do about it.

He heard Second Son's arrow whick overhead, and a dim shape among the trees flung up its hands and toppled awkwardly down and out of sight. By this time another pair came dashing toward him. He had managed to reload and he shot one.

There was no time to bring his bow into action, so he rose to his feet and met the other with his hatchet in one hand and his knife in the other. This was a strong and tricky fighter he grappled with, able to hold away his knife hand after knocking the hatchet into the rocks.

Cleve had, by now, engaged in a lot of hand-to-hand combat, but this seemed to be the hardest one yet. The Pawnee's body was greased, and even in the high country's chill he had discarded his robe and was naked to his breechclout. It was almost impossible to get a grip on him, and worse to hold him once you did.

Then he managed to get a heel behind the fellow's ankle and jerked a foot from beneath him. At the moment the warrior's weight was ill balanced, and he grabbed instinctively at Cleve to catch himself.

Cleve brought up the knife in his other hand, which was freed by the Pawnee's sudden move, and it sank into the fellow's side. The warrior gasped, his hands trying to dig out Cleve's eyes once he had his balance again. But

the wound weakened the Pawnee, and Cleve managed to
trip him again and cut his throat.

He was exhausted, breathless, but there was no time to
catch his breath. The others were coming, despite Second Son's rain of arrows among them. He noted a
feathered shaft sink into a bare chest just beyond his
barrier of rock; she was retrieving the Pawnee arrows
and returning fire with them, for these did not have the
distinctive striped turkey-feather fletching of the Cheyenne.

He gave up trying to reload. His bow was lost behind
him, but there was unlimited ammunition tumbled among
the rocks, worn shards of broken stone enough to supply
an army. Remembering his boyhood, throwing rocks
and sticks at the cattle along the Little Sac, he hefted a
palm-sized stone and let fly. A warrior went down and lay
without twitching.

Arrows sang among the stones as he ducked behind
his barrier. Cleve heaved another rock over the top
and heard a gasp from someone on the other side. He
backed quickly to the next boulder and slithered behind
it.

Something struck his back, and he looked down to see
his bow, ready-strung. He reached behind him to his
sheaf of arrows and drew the weapon, low and crosswise
as his wife's nephew had taught him to do. A dark shape
went down, and another took its place. There were too
many—it wasn't possible to take them all out, even with
two of them now firing steadily at the stealthy Pawnee.

"We must run," came Second Son's voice from above.
"Take Socks around to the other horses. I will go over
this and meet you beyond."

Cleve looked down into his son's wide dark eyes. Billy
Wolf stared back, his small face wrinkled with distress,
but he made no sound. He was either wet or frightened,

but there was no time to do anything about that. They had to get out right now.

He ducked low and led Socks around the tangle of boulders. By the time he reached the clump of loaded packhorses, Second Son was dropping from the top of the pile to join him. She was on Shadow's back as he leaped onto Socks, sheltering his son with his body. Then they were off, the horses' hooves thumping in the soft duff of the forest floor.

Arrows whizzed past. A shout of anger came to his ears, but now they were moving fast, and those behind were afoot, having left their horses behind them when they slipped up on the rockslide.

Cleve looked back for an instant, but could see no mounted figure. When he looked ahead, a dark figure came bounding across their path and sheltered behind a bush. One of those sent to flank them was waiting to head them off, Cleve realized. He tumbled off Socks and turned, just in time to receive the assault of still another Pawnee, whose well-greased body slithered in his grasp.

This was a tall man, heavy in the shoulders, strong in the legs. He toppled Cleve and they rolled together down the slope, grappling fiercely. The flint knife, which Cleve knew from old experience was sharp enough to kill him just as dead as one made of steel, kept raking at his eyes, scoring his chest, gashing his cheek.

They came to rest against the foot of a great fir tree, the hanging branches blinding him and whipping against his face and neck as he struggled. Unexpectedly, a limber branch flexed free and slashed across the Pawnee's eyes. For one instant the man was blinded, and Cleve took the opportunity to set his hands about the man's neck. With a heave and a twist he cracked the warrior's spine, and the glaring eyes went dull as he stared into them.

He rose, panting, and turned to stagger uphill toward Second Son. He found his companion standing over the body of the other warrior, wiping her own knife thoughtfully along the seam of her deerskin leggings. Without speaking, they caught the horses and mounted again.

They went down the slope when it began to ease, finding the trees thick enough to hold any arrows sent after them. Behind them Cleve heard a voice raised in a wild cry, which turned into a chant of some kind.

"That is Kills with the Lance," said Second Son, cocking her head to listen. "I have stolen many horses from his band, and I know his voice. He is angry. Very angry. He will not forget us." Her laugh was deep and completely amused.

With the lead given them by the Pawnees' need to regain their horses, they were able to move west over a ridge, leaving behind their pursuers. However, both knew that the warriors would be after them at once, and Cleve kept looking for someplace where he might set some sort of snare or obstacle to delay them still more.

They angled across a wide, sloping ledge of broken rock, keeping the horses as nearly in line as possible to avoid any unnecessary scarring of the stone. As the slope eased and they rounded the curve of the ridge, Cleve spied something ahead that promised to be useful. A nose of rock thrust out from the bedrock of the upper ridge, forcing them to cut very close beneath it because of the rough area beyond it that could endanger the legs of any horse. On top of the spur grew several pines, one of which had half fallen and was leaning against two of its fellows.

"I will set a trap," he said to Second Son, who looked at him, startled at the idea. "I'll need any line we may have left."

"There is another roll on the main packhorse," she

said. "Your old Frenchman must have spent his winters making rawhide rope, for he had much, and I brought all that was left after we tied the bales."

Cleve found what he needed and examined the path beneath the prowlike projection, once the last horse had gone past it. There was a place to set a trip rope that would be all but invisible against the pale dust and dark lines of rock. This took him only a short time to arrange.

Then he climbed the irregular knobs and jags of stone forming the nose of the obstacle and examined the trees on the top. Yes, this was a place made for such work.

While Second Son moved steadily away from their foes, he rigged a trap that even his father might have approved. Then he ran after the horses, mounted, and they rode fast along smoother ground toward another forest ahead.

Before night they had crossed so much country that both felt safe from the most persistent tracker; they had taken care to move over rocky ground or to erase signs of their passing where that was possible.

They did not pause, however, but kept on under a sky that alternated moonlight with scudding clouds, and by the time the stars began sliding down the west, Second Son agreed that they could stop to eat and rest themselves, as well as the horses.

The baby was not only wet but soiled beyond belief. Second Son washed him in a pool along the creek near their camp and packed a fresh deerhide diaper with moss carried in her pack. She had nursed the child along the way, and now she had the chance to let him drink deeply.

Then, full and clean, young Wolf Sings on the Mountain hiccuped three times and fell deeply asleep while his parents took turns watching through the night.

chapter

— 6 —

They were gone, those loaded horses, those two warriors, as if they had never been. Kills with the Lance knelt amid the duff, examining the hoof marks leading away from the rockslide, while his scouts ranged uphill and down after sign. Even as he rose, another came running from the southwest, almost straight along the mountainside, making the sign that he had found trail.

That was good. He turned to his horse, which the boy who was left to tend them had brought with the others, and sprang onto its back. Digging his heels into the animal's flanks, he tore out along the slope. Those who had been here could not be far ahead, he was sure.

Behind him the remaining members of his party followed, leaving the boy to put the dead on their mounts. He would begin the death ritual, once this task was done, as he went toward their destination, which was a summer hunting camp in the river valley.

The forest floor was scuffed where the hooves of the fugitive horses had moved. Lance had never hunted here before, so it surprised him when the ridge folded in a long curve southward.

Marks showed that his quarry had gone up and over the spine of the ridge, rather than following it around. He gestured for those nearest to follow him while others scouted to either side. Kills with the Lance was too wily a warrior to risk an ambush.

Beyond the top of the ridge lay a slope that was all rock, the soil to this windward side having been carried away by years of wind and snowmelt, leaving the underlying layer to crack and crumble. The surface was so tumbled that fresh scarring from the hooves of horses could not be distinguished from natural slips. More slips occurred even as he dismounted and padded downward, his moccasins set cautiously to avoid a fall into the ravine that lay at the lower edge of the incline.

Far below he could hear the thunder of water rushing along some hidden stream at the bottom of the unseen canyon, but he kept his gaze fixed on the ground, searching for some trace of a passing hoof. He found a crushed pebble, a scar on the upper side of an outcrop, a spot where some careless hoof had scraped over the top of a bulge of stone. They had come this way.

Signaling for two of his companions to follow him, Kills with the Lance mounted his pony and turned him along the route taken by the fugitives. As they moved around a bulge in the back side of the ridge towering above, he kept searching for further traces of his quarry, but they were very few, as if those warriors knew more than a little about covering their trail.

The slope widened, slanting steeply downward on the west, with grass now greening the scanty soil between slabs of stone. Pines began to show themselves, their skinny trunks pushing up between layers, their needles dark in the brilliant light reflected from the pale rock below them. Beyond that point the grass grew deeper as the soil layer thickened, protected by the gentler slant of the land.

There he found horse droppings and crushed grass where heavy hooves had thumped down the tender growth. Raising his hand to hurry those behind him, Kills with the Lance heeled his pony into a trot and moved forward, following the plain trail that no warrior, however skilled, could hide.

He trotted around a jutting prow of stone, his eyes intently watching the trail, and the trap, when it caught him, took him totally by surprise. His pony stumbled, going down on the left knee, and Lance was barely able to keep his seat. Then a great chunk of wood, evidently triggered by whatever tripped the horse, swung from above, smashing him off his mount and onto the hard earth below.

He lay there, stunned, tasting grit in his teeth, feeling the slow trickles of blood from forehead and shoulder and knee. Shot His Own Foot dropped beside him from the back of his paint pony and lifted the broken log so Lance could push himself clear. It was tricky work, for the rubbled area below the spur was treacherous, and neither man nor horse could be sure of his footing there.

Once upright, Kills with the Lance drew a deep breath and uttered a yell of such ferocity that even his own people flinched. He sprang onto the back of Shot His

Own Foot's pony, leaving his lamed mount behind, and rode full out after the men who had dared to trick him so slyly. They would pay!

But beyond the sloping meadow there was a tangle of ravines and forest and streams that could have hidden an entire tribe. Those he followed had chosen ways where they could conceal their tracks, or they had found a way to carry their horses through the air. He lost them thoroughly within too short a time and could not pick up the trail again, even after sending his best trackers to scout in all directions.

At last he was forced to turn back. Caked with blood, bruised and scraped, Kills with the Lance was so furious that even his best friend Many Badgers did not speak to him. Though he was a fine hunter and a leader in battle, when Lance shot sparks from his black eyes and wore a frown like a thundercloud, those who knew him left him strictly alone.

When they returned to the hunting camp, the boy had arrived before them, bringing their four dead for burial. Already their wives had slashed their faces with sharp stones and flung dust onto their heads, where it mixed with the blood into bright mud. Their plaintive wails met the returning remnants of the hunting party before they came in sight of the small valley that sheltered the few lodges.

Grimly, Lance stalked past the grieving women, the racks of drying venison and buffalo. He stepped around silent children to enter the largest lodge, where he lived with his father, Buffalo Grass, and his two wives.

Weaves Baskets met him and gestured for him to sit. She had a haunch of venison over the fire, and their two small daughters were quietly turning the meat to keep it from scorching as it hung from the tripod. The smell was good, but his gut twisted with anger and grief. The men who had died were his friends, sharers of his boyhood.

He sank wearily onto the buffalo robe spread for his use, and his father looked up from the flames. "You are angry," he said. "You found death on your hunt. I can see that you could not take vengeance upon those who killed our people."

Lance grunted, taking his daughter Smooth Dove on his lap and letting her play with the necklace of deer hooves and wolves' teeth that swung around his neck. "There is a blood debt," he said. "Two warriors, one small, the other very large. I have not seen those white men who are not Fransay that the Crow speak about, but this big one had pale hair, as they are said to do. There is war between us."

The old man's hands were busy with feathers, fletching new arrows, but now they paused. "While you were away, a Fransay came who spoke of a great gathering of white men in the south, beside the green-water river where it forks. Did your enemy go south?"

The sun had been on his right as he pursued his enemies past the trap. "Yes. South, I think, though they lost themselves among streams and forests and canyons and we could not follow them far."

"Then you may find them at that gathering. The French one who passed called it a rendezvous, in his barbaric language. If all the whites trapping for fur are to meet there, then it may be that you should go."

The wrinkled face held no expression, but there was a gleam deep in Buffalo Grass's faded eyes. He, too, was one to carry vengeance to its bitterest end, although his methods were not those that his son favored. He had taught his children and those of his peers by example, and Lance had learned that lesson well.

"We should not have come into the mountains to

hunt," Kills with the Lance said. "The buffalo cover the plain, and we could have taken meat and hides, gut and tendon enough to supply our people if we had remained there. I could have come into these places alone as I went on my medicine journey, to find the meaning of my dream."

Buffalo Grass stared across the fire, past the hanging haunch, at his son. "Your dream was a true one. I felt it when you told me of it. We all were here, in that vision, and whatever happens was meant to be. So here we are, and we will wait to see what comes. But I think you must go to the whites' rendezvous. That is part of it."

Sleep came late to the eyes of Kills with the Lance. He stared into the top of the lodge, seeing the faint sprinkle of stars beyond the smokehole, hearing the insects chirring along the stream that ran some distance from the camp. The dream came back to him so clearly that he shivered.

He had been waiting for someone, in ambush. A great eagle had stooped almost on top of him, to carry away a rabbit that screamed with the voice of a woman. Behind him his father had spoken softly, saying, "We are here among the high places for a purpose, my son. Be patient, for you will be given important signs."

But there had been no warning of death to his friends, his people. He had seen no glimpse of the tall warrior and the short one and their heavily laden horses, whose packs must hold wonderful and valuable things that his band could use.

He had not envisioned that giant yellow-haired man who grappled with Calling Bird and conquered the best wrestler among all the Pawnee. Again he shivered, thinking of the trail that disappeared so quickly and thoroughly that even his best tracker could find no trace.

He turned, his shoulder brushing that of his second

wife, Leaps Like a Rabbit, and closed his eyes. Tomorrow he would take his band, his family, and follow this stream to the river of green water. Maybe, this time, he would please his father with his deeds, though he had never entirely succeeded at that before.

He would travel down the river to the place where that fork came from the place of the setting sun. He would be there, at this rendezvous of the white men, to see what it was they did there, and to search for those who had killed his kin.

His dream had been unsettling, for there had been the feel of vast change and strange ways in his bones when he woke. Now he dreamed again, but this time his night visions were tinged with blood and darkness.

chapter
— 6 —

As they went down from the higher reaches of the mountains, along rivers watering winding valleys now lush with spring growth, Cleve found himself happier than he had been in his life. Even those first weeks with Second Son had not been more joyful.

The dangers that lurked around every bend were everyday matters, to be dealt with but not to disturb his inner well-being. The boy was growing fast, and now that it was warmer Second Son often freed him from his cradleboard and allowed him to sit before her on Shadow, his small body tucked against her belly, his dark eyes ranging over everything that came into sight.

From time to time his round face would crease into a

grin; when he frowned, his father knew to gesture downward, catching his wife's eye. Then Second Son would
change the moss in his diaper, and the small face would
smooth out and smile again.

Looking back at them, Cleve thought them the most
beautiful sight he had ever seen. Snip, who ran along-
side, silent as usual but attentive, stayed now beside
Shadow, guarding the child. Cleve was his master, but
Billy Wolf Sings on the Mountain Bennett was his small
god. Second Son he seemed to regard as something
between a force of nature, like the wind and snow, and a
part of his master.

They were going down, now, following a stream that
ultimately ran, according to Second Son, into the Green
River, which some called the Sketskedee. The forbidding slopes had shrunk away on either hand, and the
valley they now faced was alive with small game.

Rabbits and woodchucks, grouse and quail, deer and
marten and squirrels moved among the trees along the
riverbank. Some dug or browsed or picked in the deep
grass, though the day was waning and soon they would
disappear into their nightly coverts.

The horses were tired, and even Shadow's colt, Blaze,
seemed to droop with weariness. Cleve could hear their
irritable whuffs as they moved, hooves heavy on the damp
ground, but their steps picked up as they neared the
water. Ears pricked forward, eyes intent, they waited
impatiently for their riders to dismount or their lead
ropes to be loosed and then waded into the stream
and drank deeply. Small frogs leaped shrieking from the
banks and birds of many kinds protested the distur-
bance.

Before it could occur to any of the horses to try rolling
in the grass, Cleve led them some distance into a cottonwood grove to begin unloading the heavy bales. Second

Son, packing Billy Wolf into confinement once again, hung him on a nearby branch where the wind could rock him, and came to help.

The west was red with sun-shot cloud, and a wind heavy with damp swept down from the northwest, making Billy bounce on his branch and chuckle. It would rain in the night, Cleve knew as they worked to cover the bales securely.

The grove was thick, following the course of a brook. When they were done, he moved toward the concealed furs from several directions without being able to tell that the pile was there, even knowing where to look. He found their handiwork good, seemingly only a tumble of dark rocks among the bushes and trees.

When he returned to the spot chosen for camp, he found that Second Son had raised the tipi. Left to her own devices, she would, he knew, have slept beneath a cottonwood, wrapped in her blanket, but she was infinitely careful of the child. She told him frightening tales of infants taken by the coughing sickness, burning with sudden fever, and dying so quickly that the parents were left to grieve before they had had time to try healing the small one.

He helped to find deadfall among the cottonwoods. Quickly they built a fire, using shredded underbark from fallen branches. Instead of laboring with the flint and steel from Henri Lavallette's stores, they used a coal from the fire gourd that Second Son always saved from camp to camp, feeding the smolder inside with bits of twig and bark that she put into the baked mud hollow that lined the container.

When the flames leaped inside the shelter, Cleve went out again to see that the warm glow through the buffalo hides was hidden by the surrounding growth. But the grove was thick enough for concealment from all directions, and he returned, relieved, to wait; the woodchuck that Second Son had shot a few hours before was roasting already.

Outside, the rain was beginning in earnest, pounding onto the stretched hides as the wind slashed branches against the conical walls. Sputters of water dashed down the smokehole, despite the almost closed flaps whose controlling poles Second Son had arranged carefully with her eye on the direction of the wind.

Naked and happy, Billy Wolf rolled on a deerhide before the fire, and Snip nuzzled his fat stomach or touched his cold nose to the round cheek, making the child giggle. Warm light danced on their bodies and Second Son's face and the fur blankets spread for sleeping.

But Cleve knew that he would not sleep soon. They must keep watch, however safe the night might seem, with such weather sending enemies to shelter. It was when you felt safest, his wife assured him, that enemies crept close and stole your horses or counted coup upon your person. That sounded like perfect sense to him, and he belched, wiped his greasy hands on his leggings, and pulled on his robe.

This lighter one was made of deerhide, water repellent and not overly warm like the tattered cougar hide given him back in the Burning Heart village by Second Son's uncle. It flapped against him, water already streaming down, as he moved away from the tipi, going some distance into the cover of the biggest of the trees.

Now the rain didn't roar against the walls but rustled and fluttered in the leaves. The brook, some distance away, seemed to be rising, its voice growing angry as its volume increased. There was a distant mutter of thunder over the mountains to the northwest as Cleve hunkered under the curve of a deformed tree trunk, which kept the worst of the water off him.

Lightning flashed beyond the unseen heights, making the sky glow fitfully, and in a moment thunder spoke, dim with distance. Then the forked tongue sparked again, closer, and this time the thunder shook the ground. Nearer and nearer it came, like some mythic giant walking the earth, and it seemed to Cleve that the storm was making directly for this place.

He half rose, but before he could gain his feet, there came a terrific *crack-pow!* and the ground shook under his feet, throwing him back onto his haunches. Blinded by the blue-white flash, he stared toward the spot where the tipi should show a firefly glimmer through its hide walls, but the rain was now so heavy he couldn't see anything.

Then, far above the tipi, he saw a flicker of fire. Had the tree beside the tipi been struck? He shivered, sweat starting in his armpits as he made for the shelter. He had seen lightning strikes back in Missouri that had shattered huge trees into kindling wood. He had known people who were knocked into eternity between one breath and the next.

Feeling before him with his free hand, holding his knife tightly in the other in case he had to cut his way into the shelter, he followed his memory of the right direction. Then he saw the fire in the upper part of the neighboring cottonwood, the flames blown almost horizontal by the wind but the source of the fire sheltered beneath a huge chunk of wood that had been knocked loose by the bolt.

His seeking hand found the wall of the tipi, which was slick with running water, and he moved around toward the door flap, which he had fastened behind him when he came out. The shape of the tipi seemed wrong, and the door hole sagged as if the entire structure leaned toward him.

He struggled with the lacings, finally cutting them, and pulled the hide door away. "Second Son?" he called. "Snip? Billy?"

There was no sound inside. He dived through the hole and landed with his hands scorching on the hot rocks circling the firepit. The glimmer of coals seemed to be buried under ashes evidently shaken over them by the blast. In a moment he had raked them clear and fed the reborn flame with dry wood left beside the fire.

Then, with sick dread in his heart, he turned to look around the space where his family should be sleeping.

Snip was the first he saw, lying unnaturally on his side with his legs quivering. A whimper as the dog shivered convulsively and tried to get his feet under him told Cleve that he would probably be all right.

Second Son lay with the baby on her blanket. Her face was pale, her skin clammy, but she breathed. He took the child gently from her unconscious grip and felt him over. He, too, felt clammy, but he was beginning to make odd noises, shivering and squirming in his father's hands. At least he was alive. Cleve hugged him tightly, and he gasped deeply and began breathing more normally.

Cleve laid the child carefully on his own sleeping blanket, and Snip came creeping close and nestled close to him. That would keep them both more content while he saw to Second Son.

What did one do for people struck by lightning? He tried to remember what his mother had said, back there on the farm along the Little Sac. But most of those she spoke about were either dead or they had gotten up without too much trouble and gone about their business.

Well, keeping anybody warm when they were hurt was

a good thing to do. He'd seen it work with all kinds of ills and injuries. He built up the fire until it made the interior of the tipi almost too hot to bear. His heart clenched tight with hope, he watched as color came back into the faces of his wife and son and as Snip tried feebly to stand, failed, and scratched instead.

Second Son opened her eyes. *"He-est-tan-its!"* she said, her voice almost a growl. He bent over her, but her eyes, wide and dark, seemed not to recognize him. Her arm came up as if she held a knife, and he flinched backward from the threat.

She struggled to sit, her back against the slanting wall, her gaze still fixed on some dream enemy that threatened her. He knew the way she fought now, and even though she quivered as badly as Snip did, she was ready to do battle with some foe he couldn't fight for her.

Billy Wolf whimpered, and Cleve turned to the pile of infant and dog into which Snip had maneuvered him. Patting Snip absently, he lifted the baby and held him, his deerhide-and-moss diaper dripping, toward his mother.

"Wolf Sings on the Mountain needs to be changed," he said, his tone as mild as milk. Her gaze still glittered with the remnant of her vision.

"O-O-O-tan!" she said, her knife hand at the ready.

He recognized the word the Cheyenne used to name the Absaroka. She was dreaming some long-ago battle with the Crow, he knew, shocked by the lightning and somehow trapped in a vision of the past.

Now Billy Wolf was wriggling strongly, whimpering as loudly as he ever allowed himself to do. That wet diaper needed changing, and Cleve had no idea what other damage the near strike might have done the child.

"The baby!" he wheedled. "He needs you, Second Son. See, he's wet, and he's hurt."

The glitter began to fade from her eyes. "Ba-by?" she asked in English.

Cleve heaved a sigh of relief. If she was recalling his tongue, it meant she was returning from whatever past the lightning had flung her into. "Yes. Wolf Sings on the Mountain is here. He wants to suck, I think."

Now, at almost three months, the boy had already begun moving freely over the floor of the tipi, though he had not yet learned to crawl. Blindly, he turned toward his mother's voice, and doubling up his legs and pushing, he scooted toward her. Cleve was reminded of a calf finding his mother in a herd, pure instinct sending him in the right direction.

Second Son lowered her hand and shook her head as if to clear it. "Billy Wolf!" she said, reaching for the child. Then she looked up at Cleve.

"Something . . . happened."

"Yes. The lightning struck the tree beside the tipi. It shocked you or something. I was scared out of my pants, I tell you. The tipi's sagging everywhichaway, but you and the baby and Snip are all alive, and that's something."

As she bent to lift the baby she swayed. But her iron will kept her from falling as she pulled their son into her lap and bared a breast to his seeking mouth. Once he had attached himself to that source of endless comfort, Billy Wolf sighed, broke wind loudly, and relaxed.

"He is hot," she said, feeling his face and body with searching fingers.

"God, woman, we're all hot. I couldn't think of anything to do but get the tipi as warm as I could. Letting hurt folks get cold is almost always bad for them. I'm sweating like a pig myself." Cleve pushed the conical fire apart, separating it enough to lower the intensity of the flames.

He put Henri's precious iron pot into the edge of the coals and filled it with water from the skin hanging at one side of the shelter. Something else Ma did when anybody was sick was to feed them broth. It might not help, but he was damn sure it wouldn't hurt, so he shaved some of the leftover woodchuck and dropped it into the pot, along with a few wild onions and leaves Second Son had picked the evening before.

Soon the pot bubbled, and fragrant steam began to fill the place with its aroma. Snip, now less wobbly on his legs, came wagging to stand beside his master, looking up hopefully. Cleve gathered all the bones left from the hapless marmot into a pile near the door and nodded.

The dog moved with enthusiasm, though still somewhat unsteadily, to the bones and dug in, his loud crunching filling the night with added uproar, for the rain still came down relentlessly.

Cleve surveyed what might have been the scene of a disaster worse than any he had ever known. They were alive. But now he must return outside, for no matter how terrible the night, there were some enemies even more terrible. He suspected that the Pawnee Second Son called Kills with the Lance might be such a foe, who would surely not be happy at the loss of so many men at the hands of only two warriors.

The Pawnee had followed them, Cleve knew, for he had kept a watch on his backtrail. When the warrior turned homeward after losing the trail the fugitives had so carefully obscured, he must have been churning with anger.

So watch must be kept. It was never safe to congratulate yourself on escape while your enemy still lived. He covered Second Son with the fur blanket, smiling to see Billy Wolf still clinging to her breast as if it were the only security left in his small world. Cleve lifted Snip and laid the dog beside them, feeling that together they would do better than apart.

He fed the fire cautiously, for though it now could die down a bit, he didn't want his family getting chilled. The thought of trying to nurse them through pneumonia, out here in the wilderness without even a granny woman to provide herb teas, filled him with panic. He had to watch, but he wasn't going to risk them if he could help it.

When all was as good as he could make it, he bent over his wife and touched her cheek gently. Her eyes opened and she stared up blankly for a moment before coming again to her senses. "Got to go keep watch," Cleve said. "You be all right?"

She tried to smile. "We will be all right. Go, Yellow Hair. I do not trust that Pawnee not to find our trail, though we hid it well. I am not in any condition to fight him now. But wrap yourself well, for even in summer it is possible to sicken."

She was never a worrywart, and he grinned as he wrapped the still-damp robe about him and ducked again through the door flap, trying to knot the lacings together to hold it shut behind him. He would keep watch all night. By morning he hoped devoutly that things would look more promising, but something inside told him not to depend on that.

This was a cruel and unforgiving land. He was beginning to understand why the Indians seemed so stoic and unfeeling sometimes. If you let yourself care too much for anything, chances were it would be taken away. Better just to live and tend to business. Feeling too much was a sure way to get beaten to your knees.

chapter

— 7 —

His butt hurt and his head hurt, and all in all Joe Ferris felt like he'd been kicked by a mule. More than once, in fact.

It wasn't enough that his take of plews had been cut down badly when he lost one of his packhorses crossing a flooded river. It wasn't even enough that he'd run out of his carefully hoarded "medicinal" whiskey before the end of winter, leaving him nothing to do but count his many sins.

No, that was just the bad luck that followed a worse beginning. He had fallen down a mountain. It was only the mercy of God that left him alive at the end of that terrible tumble, and he could feel every spot where he'd bounced off a rock or rolled against a boulder, all the way from top to bottom of the height he called Squatting Squaw.

He should have known better than to name a mountain after any damn woman. They were the source of all evil in the world, as the Good Book plainly stated.

That mountain had done its best to kill him ever since he came to trap in the valley curving around its foot. Why he'd gone hunting for bighorn sheep up there he couldn't now say, though it had seemed a good idea at the time.

He must have gone off in the head, for he certainly didn't need the meat. It was probably just plain boredom that had driven him up the rocky slopes, his flintlock primed and ready for any shot that presented itself. By the time the snows began to melt, he'd been ready to tackle a bear or trade bites with a rattlesnake, just to break the monotony. Never again would he trap alone, that was sure.

If he had been like those other godforsaken sons of Satan he knew, he would have had a squaw with him, one who'd do the dirty work around the shanty. She might not be able to talk about religion with him, but she might have driven away the loneliness that had plagued him since the Bloods scalped his old partner and strung him up to a tree with his eyelids cut off.

Ferris had found poor Collis before he was quite dead. Cutting him down didn't do him much good. Cutting his throat was the kindest thing his partner could do, though he'd been struggling with his Bible ever since, trying to reconcile "thou shalt not kill" with the thought of leaving his friend to die long and hard with cooked eyeballs and blood-bare skull, not to mention other internal injuries that came to light when Ferris moved his body to the grave he'd dug.

Old Joe spat thoughtfully into a curve of dingy snow on the shady side of a pine tree and kicked his heels into his horse, Tarnation's, sides. He didn't like thinking about that time or the limp way his friend's body had dragged across the ground, as if he hadn't a bone left that wasn't broke.

He shook himself. If he couldn't find another white-man partner, even if those tended to be fornicators and drunkards, he'd just go without. And if the time ever came when he danced naked through the trees, entirely off his head with solitude, then that was just the way the Good Lord saw fit to make it happen.

He wouldn't take up with a red-tail wench, no matter what. No matter what dreams he had . . . again he shook himself.

It had been fifteen years since his Mattie died back in the east, and he'd only visited *white* whores since then. Red ones he would not tolerate. But it was years since he'd been in St. Louis . . . he kicked the sorrel mare again and rode forward, head down, eyes seeing inside his soul instead of watching the trail.

And that was no sensible way for a seasoned mountain man to travel.

Tarnation gave a terrified whinny and reared, almost unseating him. If he hadn't been so strung about with his pack and rifle and odds and ends, he would have sailed off the horse's back, but as it was, he grabbed onto his blanket roll with one hand and a strap with the other. Then he had to grip with his knees and pray harder than he had for some time, because Tarnation took off up a rocky stream bed, splashing and clattering as she fled the she-grizzly that had reared up ahead of them on the trail.

He could hear the packhorses whinnying fearfully and the clatter of their hooves behind his mount as they followed his sorrel's lead.

"Whoa!" Ferris roared. "Whoa, damn you!" He grabbed the reins, knotted loosely and held under his knee, and hauled the horse down to a scramble.

Bouncing and cursing, he managed to stop the beast. "You wall-eyed, no-good, bang-tailed piece of carrion!" he said between his teeth. "You been seein' griz for years now. We wasn't near enough for her to worry about us, and I didn't see no cubs nearby, neither. You just wanted to run off, didn't you, and leave me spittin' dust!"

He managed to turn her and block the flight of the packhorses. Aching in every joint and muscle, he dismounted painfully and caught all the animals, stringing them together on his picket line, five packhorses loaded to the gills with beaver. Even without the sixth, this was a good haul.

Collis would have loved this rendezvous idea, getting together with others, swapping lies, drinking himself senseless every night. He'd have tumbled every red wench he saw and those he didn't see would've come after *him*. He'd been a fair hand with the women, and that had given them some great arguments on bitter winter nights.

Collis certainly would have gotten better prices for their plews than Ferris would, not to mention doing things his partner would never have risked his immortal soul to do. What a shame he hadn't lived to see it.

He had the horses secured between two trees now, and he left Tarnation to cool her heels while he crept back down the stony creekbed to see if the cause of all the commotion had decided to amble on out of the way. She was grunting and snuffling under a log, digging out grubs, it looked like.

She reminded him of his grandma, who'd raised him, working and talking to herself around the dip of snuff she kept in her lip. He could understand just about as much of the bear's talk as he had Grandma's. He'd had many a whaling because he misunderstood her mumbled orders.

Knowing that this would take a while, he moved back up the runnel and sat under a clump of young aspens, watching the woods for any sign of trouble. With this run of luck, there had to be something bad just around the corner. He thought of Job and took out his worn Bible.

That reminded him of the man who had taught him the fear of God. William Kelly. Skinny drink of water with a voice that you could cut down trees with, if you turned him sideways. To his great shame, Joe had helped his enthusiastic companions hoist the self-appointed preacher into a tree in the middle of a blizzard and leave him there all night, naked as a rock.

When you're young, he thought, *you don't think about such things as eternal damnation. I was just as wore out with his long-winded sermons as the rest, and if I'm honest, I have to admit that. I wanted to drink and fornicate with anything that would hold still, just like the rest of 'em.* Being without Mattie after three years of marriage hadn't helped, either.

He opened the book, but his mind rambled on, remembering Holy William. The scene was as clear as if he was still there in the clearing around their cramped shanty, cheering on the ones who were letting the blue and goose-pimpled body of the preacher down from the tree where he had spent the night.

As he hit the ground Curg Moore turned him over with his foot and stared down into the narrow face. "We done put up with your pious talk and your holy ways till we're plumb tired to death," he told the preacher.

William tried to answer him, but his teeth were chattering so hard he couldn't say a word, which was the first time any of them could recall that happening. Curg kicked him again, and the shivering man moved stiffly to grab the leather shirt and pants Joe put out for him.

They didn't want him dead—quite—but they sure as hell wanted him gone.

Once the shaking man had dressed himself and wrapped a worn buffalo robe around his shoulders, Curg brought out all his plunder and laid it on the ground beside the sorriest horse in their string. Nobody wanted to be called a thief, so most of the things were Kelly's own, and some were even donations from men who felt guilty about what they were doing. Joe's own second-best hunting knife was in the pile, so he knew.

Ferris shivered, though the sun was warm on his back as he sat, remembering the way Kelly had risen, his teeth still clacking, and loaded the equipment onto the horse. By the time that was done, effort had warmed him a bit, and he turned to face them, after struggling into the saddle.

"You don't know what you're doin," he had said. "I'll forgive you, or try to, like the Man did on the cross. Maybe I won't get there soon, but I'll manage it before I die. But you're goin' to get older and think about what you done here yesterday and today. Then it's goin' to come home to you, and you're goin' to feel like yellow dogs."

Joe Ferris, only twenty-one then, had moved up beside the horse, the seeds of guilt already working in him. "I'm already sorry, Bill. You've been a pain in the ass, but nobody deserves what we done to you. You got my second-best knife. Now I want you to have my extra moccasins. You'll need them, I imagine, before you're done."

He tucked the footgear under the strap holding the bedroll behind the saddle, and Kelly looked down at him, his pale eyes deep with pain. "Then I'll give you somethin', too," the preacher said.

He reached behind him and fumbled in the pack he

had so painfully assembled. A tattered Bible came out of its depths. It wasn't the one Joe recognized.

"I got a extra Bible. You take it. Then when you start dreaming about this day, you get it out and read it. Maybe you'll take my place, in time, and do the work I tried to do. I admit maybe I done it bad, because I ain't a educated man and don't know much about such things. I appoint you, Joe Ferris, to look after these men's souls."

Tarnation snorted and danced, and Ferris came out of his dream of the past. It had been as if Kelly had transferred something of his mission when he handed down that old Bible. Joe had never let himself get carried away like Kelly did, so he didn't irritate his companions so much, but he'd studied that book from cover to cover many times since that day.

After he split off from the bunch to go his own way, he'd had a number of partners. Collis had been the last of a long series, and every one of them had come to rely on his advice and his word. He'd been careful not to make them mad at him, just because Bill had showed him the way *not* to do his work.

No, he'd learned a lot from Kelly about how not to convert heathen. That was why he had such good relations with his trapping buddies, as well as all the Indian tribes he'd had dealings with. Only a few individuals had gotten crossways with him, and he avoided them all he could.

Tarnation stamped, looking down the hill. She knew, that crazy sorrel mare, that the sow bear had moved, he reckoned. He clucked to her, unstrung the rope from the tree and led the line of horses down again to the trail he must take over this mountainside and down into the valley beyond. He was headed for Henry's Fork, and he'd get there if every bear and every cougar and every bloodthirsty Blood or Crow or Shoshonni in the country stood in his way.

The sun had moved over the mountain now, and he was in shadow from the trees along the trail. He kept his mind on his work, this time, because he wanted no more bad luck. For a God-fearing man, he'd had more than his share, this season. His bruises ached, too, and he groaned softly as he mounted Tarnation and set off to the southeast, toward the Green and the rendezvous.

chapter

— 8 —

Second Son was never quite at ease in mountainous country. She had been born in the wide stretches of the plains, her gaze used to traveling unimpeded to the edges of the sky. The tops of ridges, with their wide sweeps of visible country, were exhilarating, but once the train of horses moved down again into forests or ravines, she felt as if she were boxed in a trap.

Now, trailing behind the string, she felt a sudden revulsion at the tunnel of trees through which they were riding. It was too like the place she had seen in a medicine dream, years ago when she was on the edge between her childhood and becoming a warrior. The memory of the terror she had felt in that dream still shook her, and she kicked her moccasined heels into Shadow's sides and crowded close to the last packhorse in the line.

Cleve, riding ahead with Billy Wolf on his back in his cradleboard, emerged from the darkness of the tree tunnel into a shaft of sunlight, and the brightness turned his hair to gold. She smiled, pushing away the last of the feeling that dream memory always gave her. No Cheyenne warrior would dream of carrying the infant on his back, but Yellow Hair seemed to enjoy being close to his son.

Snip ran beside his master's horse, looking up from time to time to be certain his baby was quite safe. The devotion of the dog to "his" people was something that still amazed Second Son.

Beyond the shadowy track was a long stretch of rocky slope, slanting from left to right and running down to a steep canyon at the bottom of which she could hear rushing water. The trail that followed the lip of the canyon was too stony to take tracks, but her quick eyes found a pile of half-dried droppings off to one side, and she knew that other horses had gone this way within the past day.

She saw Cleve turn and signal, and she knew that he, too, had seen the sign and wanted to consult with her about reading it. Something ahead of him was of interest, for he dismounted and motioned for her to do the same.

She dropped from Shadow's back and moved forward, reassuring the packhorses with a word as she passed each one. Then she knelt beside Cleve. Printed clearly into a scatter of horse dung were two moccasin tracks. Familiar ones.

"Pawnee," she said. "This is not their usual hunting ground, but those are Pawnee moccasins. See the way they were cut." She traced the distinctive elements of the print, and Cleve nodded.

"I thought so. They're ahead of us, then. You think they're the same ones we met back on the other side of the mountain?"

She squatted easily, her eyes examining the trail ahead and behind, the sky above, the canyon to their right, and the rocky expanse to their left. There was no physical sign, other than the dung and the tracks, but she was listening to the wind, the cries of an eagle circling high overhead, the very voices of the scrub growing along their route.

She was smelling the faintest remnant of the Pawnees' distinctive scent, mixed with the dry acridness of manure. Every instinct she possessed told her that Kills with the Lance had come this way.

"Not many Pawnee come into the mountains. Not many of the Tsistsistas, either, though we hunt here more than they. If we met one hunting party and it was that led by Kills with the Lance, then this track was made by his group or some others belonging to those of his band who have come into the high country. This is either that warrior or his kin. I am sure of that." She rose decisively and looked down again at the track.

"We do not want to leave so clear a trail. Go ahead, and I will come behind, brushing away all sign that anyone has come this way. If there are others behind us, in the village to which Kills with the Lance belongs, they might send another group in this direction. They might even be going to the rendezvous, as we are. The Pawnee are great traders."

Cleve glanced up, his eyes bright and intense. "If this get-together is going to work for Ashworth at all, it's going to have to be a rendezvous under some kind of truce. Will the Pawnee observe that?"

She nodded. "The Pawnee are honorable people. They abide by treaties. They live by the rules of their tribe. But they are very old enemies of the Tsistsistas, and we must take care not to taunt them with our escape. That would abuse the hospitality of your friend Ashworth."

She turned back and slapped Shadow sharply on the rump. The mare followed the other horses as Cleve led them forward, leaving Second Son to gather fallen branches of brush and whisk the telltale prints away, along with the shreds of dried manure. The rock showed no sign of her passing, when she checked closely, and at last she caught up with the string, which Cleve had led down a narrow ravine to the edge of the water far below.

The sun was now down behind the mountains to the west, and shadows had engulfed the slope along which they had traveled. With Pawnee ahead and possibly behind, it might be as well to camp for the night. When Second Son made the suggestion, Cleve agreed; they watered the animals, filled their own waterskins, and moved back up the ravine. They traveled a mile or so farther along the edge of the canyon and climbed the slope, searching for a hidden spot in which to camp.

There was a formation towering beside a cliff, like a spur of yellowish stone. A more uninviting place was hard to imagine, but behind it was a sheltered nook large enough for a dry camp without fire. The horses must get by on what little leafage they could munch from the small aspens growing up the slope behind. After sniffing around the area thoroughly, Snip lay down and panted his approval.

Second Son took Billy Wolf from his cradleboard and suckled him while she chewed a strip of jerky. She felt strange, and the picture of that tree tunnel still hung behind her eyes. Even when she was rolled in her blankets, she was haunted by that unwanted memory, and her sleep was filled with unwelcome dreams.

Singing Wolf, her brother, was calling across the prairie, his voice rising and falling like that of his namesake, the lone wolf that sang to the moon. He was warning her, she knew, but she could not quite understand his words as the song quavered through the spring wind.

She was riding very fast, after a wounded buffalo, guiding her horse with her knees, holding her bow ready for the fatal shot. Once she came close, and the beast turned its massive head and stared into her eyes. Its own eyes were scarlet; there was slaver about its mouth, and its curly coat shone with a frozen sheen like ice.

It ran into the mouth of a canyon that grew deeper and deeper until the walls seemed to close overhead, but she thundered on after the beast. It was like a tunnel, she thought, or a cave.

She took the single rein from beneath her knee and tried to slow her horse . . . not Shadow, she noted with dismay, but a roan with a vicious eye circled in white and a mouth made of iron. A lark's-head knot secured her line to its lower jaw, but all her tugging could not succeed in slowing the horse.

Instead, it bent its neck, bringing its head about, and one wild eye stared into hers as the beast galloped forward, blind to what might lie ahead. If the buffalo found a place to turn, they would be trapped here, and the horse would plunge onto the waiting horns. Both would die.

She slung her bow over her back while the wind whipped her hair and sang shrilly in her dangling eagle feathers. Leaning forward, she put her hands on either side of the horse's neck, soothing the maddened animal.

"Slow, my little one. Stop, my little one. Now." But the roan pounded forward still, and now the canyon tunnel was dark, and she could no longer see her quarry as it ran ahead of them toward whatever end there might be.

Second Son moaned and struggled to waken, knowing

that this was a dream but unable to escape its grip on her sleeping mind. She turned, touched Cleve, who was watching beside her, and half woke; the dream pulled her back and back until she was again in that tunnel.

But now she was afoot, with Billy Wolf riding her back. She was running forward along a slippery track, trying to check her speed, almost falling at every bend in the long, black corridor. And then she came around a knee of rock to see light ahead, gleaming coldly. At last she was able to stop herself by catching a protrusion from the wall, and she stood, swaying and spent, staring at the thing that stood at the blank end of the tunnel.

This was an old bull, shaggy, tough, and cruel. Those eyes still shone red in the light, which seemed to be coming from the silvery mist that surrounded him. His coat was now almost blinding in its shining mantle of frost, and his breath steamed as he panted, snorted, and pawed at the rocky ground.

Second Son reached for her bow, but her seeking hand found only the edge of the cradleboard. She felt for her hunting knife, but it had been lost in that terrible flight, and she found instead the short, wide-bladed one the women used for skinning out the warriors' kill.

That shocked her, for she had never owned one. It had been her kill that the women flayed and gutted. Yet at this moment when she needed more than ever before to use the arms and the skills of her training as a man, she seemed left with only herself and the wits and nerve of a woman.

If that bull charged, she could never outrun him up that slick surface. Her son would be trampled and gored, and their blood and bones would mix together on this stony ground, leaving Yellow Hair to grieve.

Fury filled her. A warrior needed no weapons. At her side, forgotten, perhaps, by the god who sent this dream, hung her coup stick. If she and Billy Wolf must die, then it would be as warriors, not as fugitives.

Second Son filled her lungs and roared her rage into the

night. She raised the coup stick and stood facing the terrible buffalo, which snorted again as if questioning this crazy woman challenging him on his own ground.

Billy Wolf made a soft sound. It was not a whimper but almost a word, as if even the child agreed with her decision.

She pushed herself off from the rock she had clutched and shot forward toward the astonished animal. The bull flinched backward, its hindquarters hitting the wall behind with a thump and a soft clatter of falling debris.

Second Son crossed the few yards separating them and struck that broad face between the eyes, just below the wickedly curved horns. "I count coup!" she shouted.

Something was tugging at her. Billy Wolf? No, he was too small. But she was drawn backward, away from the image of the bull, which was still frozen with astonishment, back into the night, where she lay beside Cleve with Billy Wolf between them.

"Here, you're having one hell of a nightmare," he said, shaking her shoulder. "What were you dreaming, anyway?"

Second Son gave a sigh that was almost a sob. Even as she was pulled out of the dream the buffalo changed, his bulk shrinking, and before she woke fully, she saw in the animal face the sharp black eyes of Kills with the Lance.

"A medicine dream," she gasped. "A terrible one, Yellow Hair. We must guard ourselves. We must watch our son closely. There is a threat, and my brother, out on the plain with the great summer hunt of our people, has dreamed it, too. He called to me, warning. . . ."

Cleve's warm arms went around her, holding her close as she huddled the baby to her breast. "Tell me," he said.

"A medicine dream is for the dreamer. Only if it affects the welfare of the tribe do I tell it to others. This may trouble you."

"Tell me," he said again, and this time she nodded against his chest and told him what she had seen in her sleep. As she finished describing the vision she added, "There will be danger in a dark place. I saw a terrible buffalo, an old bull with red eyes and ice on his back, and he was not like any of his kind that I have ever known. At the last he became Kills with the Lance."

She felt her husband's arms tighten on her shoulders, as if he were shocked by something she had said. She moved to loose herself and look into his eyes.

"I think you had dreams for both of us," Yellow Hair said. "For I had a vision, years ago while I was with Ashworth's men wintering on the Missouri.

"I saw that buffalo, the same one I am sure, on a frozen morning with ice on his back and fire in his eyes. He snorted steam and I knew that he was my own private totem. An evil one! I've never told anyone about this before, but now you've seen him for yourself."

She shivered and pulled her robe closer about her neck. "I never was a woman before," she said, "unarmed and on foot, with a baby to protect. As a warrior I had no understanding of this, though we protect the women and children with our lives."

Yellow Hair touched Billy Wolf's dark hair with one finger. "Your part of the dream was strange. Do you think it was to show you what it's like to be a woman? Not many people have the chance to be a man and a woman at the same time, and maybe that's what it tried to tell you."

Second Son thought about this for a moment. Was there some part of her that had resisted all thought of being female, past the obvious ones of loving her husband and bearing her child? And might another part of her need to understand herself as a female? But that was too complicated, and she shook herself and rose.

"Dreams are not always what they seem to be, though there is usually truth to be found. But the east is showing a line of light, and we should move. Instead of following the stream below the canyon rim, I think we should climb this ridge and move along its top, keeping watch on both sides and never showing ourselves on the sky-line."

The going was rough, and as the day passed they took turns afoot, scouting the descending slopes on either side of the twisting spine of rock and forest along which they moved. This was slower traveling than that on the game trail, but before noon Cleve returned to the horses, moving cautiously along a patch of weathered rock.

"There's an ambush down there," he said. "I think Pawnee, and that ought to be Kills with the Lance. Do you suppose he had somebody watching his backtrail and spotted us before we left the track?"

"He is a wary warrior," she said. "If a scout took word of our coming to him, he would find a promising place and wait for us to arrive. But one scout cannot be in two places, so he doesn't yet know we are not walking into his hands. We will drop down the farther side of the ridge for a time and move as fast as possible, before he realizes we are not coming."

Cleve nodded. They led the animals quietly down-slope, keeping in the thickest patches of trees, and before long they found another game trail leading downward toward the southeast. Only the tracks of small animals marked it, except for one great hoofprint of an elk, and Second Son was confident that men had not walked this way in some time.

If her instinct was correct, this would lead them down to the desert country very near the Sketskedee, and from there it would be only a fairly short journey to the joining of streams the white men called Henry's Fork.

They went quietly, keeping Snip very close, watching the horses for signs that they might sense the nearness of others of their kind. But all was quiet, and in time they descended the last slope onto a stretch of high desert that was well grown with sagebrush.

This was both a relief and a worry. They could see any enemy for long distances, but enemies, in turn, could see them as well. For that reason Second Son dismounted, and Cleve followed her example. The horses showed up all too plainly, with their tall burdens of bales, but with riders the mounts would have been even more noticeable.

It was slower than riding, of course, but in time they came within sight of the long line of cottonwoods and willows that marked the river. Without words they turned the line of horses southward, paralleling the course of the stream, for both knew that others would also be going toward the rendezvous, and two people might not be able to protect their valuable plews from raids, if the like of Jules Terrebonne traveled toward the fork.

Keeping the distant line of mountains on the west and the jagged silhouettes of heights ahead, they had no trouble finding the rendezvous. Before they reached the first of the low hills flanking the fork, another company of travelers came into view.

They first appeared as specks in the distance, their route converging with that of her own party. Snip growled, his hackles rising, but Cleve quieted the dog and began to grin. Second Son realized rather sadly that he had missed having one of his own kind with him since the death of Holy William, however strong his feelings for her and Billy Wolf.

When they got within hailing distance, Cleve sprang onto Socks and kicked him in the ribs. "Yaeeeehah!" he yelled, taking off toward the line of laden horses and the three mounted men. "Hey, you fellows! Americans?"

She walked along beside Shadow, her hand touching her child's cheek. His round eyes stared curiously out at the world, and only when he learned to talk could she expect to know what he thought of the place into which he had come. It was a comfort to have him there while her man rode away to find other company than hers.

But she was not a jealous person, and her warrior training had taught her to control her emotions to the point at which she often seemed to have none. Instead of reacting, she mounted Shadow with Billy Wolf tied onto her back again and trotted forward, leading the string of packhorses.

The distant line of men and animals had come to a halt, waiting for Cleve's arrival. When Socks thudded up, they seemed excited, waving their arms, reaching forward to shake Yellow Hair's hand in the way of white men, raising their voices in the meaningless syllables that Cleve had told her were curses, though why the whites cursed their friends she had never been able to decide.

When she came up to the other string, she politely fell behind it with her own pack animals, letting Cleve determine their relationship with this new group. She had known only a few whites—Jules Terrebonne, who had been her enemy but was now dead. Henri Lavallette, who had been Cleve's friend and her enemy; he, too, was dead, by her hand.

And Cleve Yellow Hair, her "wife," won fairly in battle. He had warned her, on their long journey to the rendezvous, that white men were not all like him or like the Frenchmen, either. She smiled, falling back farther to escape the dust from the beasts before her, thinking of his efforts to make her understand his people.

They had been camped under a rocky outcrop, their fire already snuffed for the night. Cleve had taken her hand in the darkness and stroked it as he tried to explain to her the strange word *lie* that he kept repeating.

"Second Son, I know now, because you've taught me, that your people don't even have a word for not telling the truth. They don't have a word for truth either, that I've discovered, because they just know what is without worrying about making up something that isn't."

"Buy why should anyone do that?" she had asked him. "There is no good to be had from things that never happened."

He sighed into the darkness, his breath a gust of frustration. "I know it's hard. I never knew, back in Missouri, that there was anybody, anyplace, who didn't lie. Pa lied. Even Ma lied sometimes, to protect her young'uns. *Everybody* lied, even the preacher, I've found out since. So I had just as much trouble understanding that your people *don't* lie as you're having getting it into your head that mine *do*."

She had thought carefully about the things he had told her in the seasons of their marriage. Dimly she began to realize that this was the hardest thing she would ever do, harder than counting coup, fourth in turn, upon a well-armed enemy. Harder than leaving her people to follow this stranger.

"You say to me that all of your people do not say what is real. Always?"

"No, not always. That's what makes it so hard. If you knew never to believe anything a white man says, that would be easy. You'd know just what to do. But sometimes they are perfectly accurate and say exactly what's on their minds without a hitch.

"Other times, when they want something from you that you don't want to give or to do, they'll just say anything at all to persuade you to do what they want. And not a word of it means anything at all."

She had frowned into the darkness, trying to understand. "But why do you not give people what they want? Among my people we make gifts all the time—horses, weapons, furs, and food. When there is need, we give. Why do your people not do the same?"

Cleve seemed to think a long while, his breathing slow, his body relaxed beside her. Then he said, "Because my people want a lot of things they don't need. A lot of things they have no business wanting, in fact. Henri, for instance, wanted you. That wasn't his right, and you defended yourself from him, as you should have.

"There may be others, there at the rendezvous, who'll try the same thing. But you're a warrior, and you can do whatever it takes to set them straight, even if it means killing them. They're grown men, and if they want to take chances with their lives, it's their business.

"But others may try other things. It's hard to say what, but don't you agree to do anything, to take a gift or to give anything until you talk it over with me. I don't want my own people to hurt you. I don't intend for that to happen. All right?"

Shadow snorted at the thick dust of the trail, bringing her out of the memory, and Second Son heeled her out of the line, taking the string of animals to the right and away from the irritation. She watched the men ahead, still slapping backs and talking very loudly in their uncouth tongue.

She wondered what would happen when many of that kind got together. Would there be Tsistsistas and Lakota, Absaroka and Pawnee there as well? She had never been in such a mixed group of peoples, and her heart quickened at the thought of the strange things she was about to see and hear and learn.

Her son was not the only one entering a new world, eyes and ears wide open and hungry for information.

They traveled now in company with this new party. At the end of the day, Yellow Hair took her to meet these three pale-eyed men, and even her stout heart beat a bit faster at the thought of speaking with them. She was very quiet as they approached; her eagle feathers were carefully erect in her hair, her best robe folded precisely about her shoulder.

"This is my partner," Cleve said to the tallest of the men. "And my wife. She's not what you might think, so be careful. A Cheyenne warrior isn't somebody you want to get on the bad side of." He laughed to take the sting from his words, and Second Son saw the three sets of eyes slide sideways to examine her from head to foot.

She was glad that she had dressed in her best warrior garb: the fine deerhide shirt and leggings, the breechclout that marked her as a man, the throat-to-navel ornament formed of fine bones and bright quills that her sisters-in-law had made for her after her first raid. She knew that she did not look like any woman these strangers had seen among her own kind.

She gazed back at them, her expression enigmatic, her arms folded formally. Cleve turned to her and said, "Second Son, this is Edward Fellmore. The skinny fellow here is Tom Carson, and that other one over there feeding his face is Lee Pulliam. They're going to rendezvous, and it looks as if they did real well, too."

The three men seemed puzzled as to how to greet her. Fellmore rose and looked down at her, his grizzled brows meeting over his large red nose. "Glad to have you, ma'am. Uh—Miz Second Son. We've heared about your man. Word got all over the mountains, seems like, that he kilt a bear with nothing but a ax, back east a ways. Emile Prevot keeps tellin' that tale everywhere he goes, to everybody he sees.

"That Frenchy thinks old Cleve Bennett is dead. It's goin' to be a rare treat to see his expression when he comes face-to-face with him." Fellmore's leathery cheeks creased in a wide grin, and he held out a hand awkwardly.

She had watched as the white men greeted each other, and she extended her own hand as she had seen the others do. His grip was hard, but hers was like iron; his squeeze met equal pressure. The pale eyes widened the slightest bit, and she knew she had surprised him.

"He-lo," she said, keeping her voice low and calm. "I am glad to meet with you."

The other two men nodded, their faces guarded. It was plain that they didn't know what to make of an Indian woman who was a warrior and a wife. To ease their awkwardness, she sank onto her heels beside their fire, leaving Cleve to carry on the conversation.

"We got a boy, just a few months old. He's back with Snip, my dog. That damn dog thinks the baby belongs to him, and anybody trying to bother the camp would get a real shock."

She could hear in Yellow Hair's voice a note of boyishness that she had never heard there before. He had come to her people after terrible trials, old before his time. Now she knew that he had become a man almost before he had the time to be a boy.

The few times he had talked to her about his father, she had been shocked and sickened. Her people did not abuse children. Forcing a small one to work as hard as a grown-up, without kindness and without praise, not to mention beating him, was something she could not forgive.

She sat silent, listening to the voices more than to the words. Much of what the white men said was unintelligible to her, but she watched the faces in the ruddy firelight, seeing in these bearded men a spark of the same youthfulness that Yellow Hair was revealing. Were all white men boys at heart?

Her own people were great ones for jokes and pranks, and laughter was a part of life, even in the hardest of times. But she was beginning to believe that though these big fellows roared with laughter and talked loudly and cheerfully, they were not a happy people.

chapter

— 9 —

Cleve had thought he was perfectly contented with his life. His wife, his son, the rich harvest of furs from both Lavallette's store and their own efforts seemed to add up to more than he ever would have dreamed of when he left Missouri. It didn't occur to him that he was missing his own sort of people.

But the sight of these roughly dressed men in their tatterdemalion mix of deerhide shirts, animal-skin caps, and the remnants of woolens and flannels brought a lump to his throat. Their reddened faces, cracked and lined with sun and wind, were those of his own breed.

From their reaction when he came galloping up on Socks, he thought they, too, were glad to see another white face. The tall, chunky man who had first reined in his horse rode back to meet him.

"Ed Fellmore," he said, reaching across the space between their mounts to take Cleve's hand. His grip was like the jaws of a bear, but Cleve found to his glee that he was able to match squeeze for squeeze, and neither was able to gain the mastery.

By that time the other two had halted their string of horses and now they rode back to join their companion. The wizened little fellow, almost as skinny as Holy William had been, introduced himself as Tom Carson, and the taller man said only, "Lee Pulliam," as he sat back, took an old clay pipe from some recess in his clothing, and watched this unexpected meeting.

"Headed for rendezvous?" asked Carson. "I kin see you are, from that fat haul of plews you're carryin'. This was one fine idea that man Ashworth come up with. Them tradin' forts was eatin' us up alive."

Fellmore spat into the dust of the track they had made. "Nothin' says this here rendezvous won't do the same thing," he said. "You haul goods away out here to hell and gone, it stands to reason the trader's going to make a killin'. But better a new thief than the old ones, I say. At least we'll see some new faces. Like yourn."

Cleve turned to wave Second Son on after them. Then he pulled Socks into formation with the others so they could talk without shouting.

"I started out here with Ashworth's bunch," he said. "Left in the summer of twenty-one, but we didn't get too far before we lost our horses and had to fort up for the winter. Then the next summer we ran into hostiles and I got split off from the rest. Been on my own, more or less, ever since."

"See you got a partner," said Pulliam. "You trust an Indian?"

Cleve felt a big grin forming inside him. He would have some fun with these fellows, before he was done. There was no way to know from her dress or her attitude that Second Son wasn't a man, and he thought there was room for humor in the situation.

"This one I trust," he said, without expanding on the relationship. "I had one white partner that couldn't be trusted, back a ways, but that came to a sudden end. I got his plews on the horses, along with ours. Together they come to a nice batch."

Carson heeled his horse into a lope and headed a straying pack animal back into line. He yipped like a whole tribe of the Tsistsistas, Cleve thought, before he was satisfied and turned again to the tight group of riders.

"Camp by us tonight," Fellmore said. "It's good to get some new tales after starin' at each other's ugly faces for two years. You kin even ask your Indian pard to join us, if you want. He talk English?"

"Even some French," said Cleve. "They been here so long, I guess most of the tribes have learned some of their lingo, just to get by. The one who taught Second Son French was a fellow name of Lavallette. Henri Lavallette. You ever hear of him?"

It was time to get some idea of how Henri had been regarded by other trappers. Maybe he would decide to tell just what happened to the old Frenchy and maybe not. It would depend on the gist of conversations like this one.

Pulliam snorted. "I spent a winter along the Belle Fourche three—no, four winters past. Henry'd come back to trap his old streams, and I run into him and kept him comp'ny for the season. I'd had bad luck. Lost most of my gear and horses fording a river in flood and he taken me in and worked my tail off."

"Did he pay you in traps and gear?" asked Cleve, wondering how the old man could have kept so much in store if he had stocked occasional wanderers like Pulliam and himself.

Pulliam laughed, his expression taut and humorless. "He give me some grub, some old traps that didn't work worth a damn, and a lot of advice, most of which was good. The best was, 'Don't trust nobody you meet out here until you know him mighty well.'"

"That sounds like him," said Cleve. "Only he'd have said, 'Nevair trust the man until you know him ver' well.' I spent some time with him myself, after I got loose."

Fellmore spat again. "Damn Frenchies are slippery as mice. I never found one I could cheat, and I tried almighty hard."

It looked hopeful, Cleve decided. Once they were all settled into camp at rendezvous, he would tell the tale of Henri's demise with ruffles and flourishes, if the consensus among his peers was much the same as this.

The day passed quickly, and he knew Second Son was following, though she had moved out of the dust and was paralleling their track. When his companions stopped for the night beside a runnel that was still partially filled with runoff from the distant mountains, and started unloading their horses, he turned back toward the nearby cluster of his own animals.

Second Son was building a fire in the shelter of a big rock. Billy Wolf was propped in his cradleboard against the boulder, his black eyes dancing in the flickers of the blazing tinder. Snip came lolloping toward his master, his tongue hanging out, his tail busy.

"You could've come on up with us," he said as he squatted beside his wife and helped fan the flames. "But I'm glad you didn't. I'm going to have some laughs tonight when we go over and I introduce you to 'em. They won't know what to make of you."

She glanced up, her eyes veiled, but he thought it was the smoke that made her look so odd. "You will laugh at me?" she asked, her tone guarded.

Cleve felt a pang of guilt. He had turned his back on her as if she had ceased to exist, depending on her at the same time as he was ignoring her. He didn't know much about women, but even he understood that this might not be the smart thing to do.

"No, I'm going to laugh at *them* when they find out this great warrior is a woman and I'm her wife." He reached for her hand and held it warmly between his. "Your folks like a good joke, I know, because I've seen many a prank and many a laugh while I stayed with your brother. This'll be something to tell them about when we visit the Burning Hearts again."

Her expression eased, and her dark eyes reflected warm lights from the blaze, which was leaping among dried twigs from the cottonwoods and willows and flat plates of dried buffalo dung. The slight dimple at the corner of her mouth deepened, and he knew she was fighting a smile that threatened to break her solemnity.

"You will tell them who I am?" she asked.

He nodded. "We'll leave Billy Wolf here with Snip. Near enough to hear if anything should bother him, but far enough so that they won't suspect we've got a young–'un. Dress up in your best—that white robe with the fancywork, and the quilled moccasins and the long bone necklace your sister-in-law gave you. Look like a great chief! I want their jaws to drop."

She stood, leaving him to tend the pot in which strips of jerky simmered with random leaves she had picked from the summer growth as they walked the horses on the flatland. He knew she would take pains to resemble the great chief she had it in her to be, if the occasion ever arrived.

She returned in splendor, her eagle feathers crisply erect in her glossy hair, her moccasins soft as butter on her narrow feet. The pale deerhide robe, the bright quills and dyed bones of the long neckpiece glimmered in the firelight, turning her into a commanding figure. He hurried to eat his supper and to hold the baby after the child suckled so Second Son could eat hers, being careful not to spot the pale leather of her robe.

They allowed Billy Wolf to crawl about on a hide blanket for a bit as Snip nosed him and let the baby pull his ears and bat at his waving tail. Then they packed him back into his cradleboard and settled him onto the top of the pile of bales, facing the fire, and sat until his eyes closed and his small head sagged sideways against the padding. Snip lay at the foot of the pile, his nose on his tail, his ears alert for anything that might come.

By then it was clear that the men around the nearby campfire were finished with their own meal. When Fellmore hailed him, Cleve rose and yelled, "Ready for company?"

"Sure are," came the reply. "Got fresh coffee made, too."

He turned to Second Son. "Let's go, Tsistsistas Warrior. I can hardly wait to pull their legs."

He could see in the three grubby faces, as they approached the fire, that Fellmore, Carson, and Pulliam were impressed with the dignity and bearing of his companion. Few Indians of their experience, Cleve was sure, were as imposing as this one. With pride, he saw the calm grace with which his wife stood waiting while they gazed at this unexpected vision of warlike splendor. Nothing indicated that this could possibly be a woman.

When he introduced her, he could hardly keep his

face straight, for sheer shock traveled around the arc of faces. Carson swallowed a gulp of overhot coffee and almost choked. Pulliam sat up straight, his eyes wide. But Fellmore was a stout fellow and he rose at last to greet this unusual visitor.

Now Carson was blank-faced; Pulliam grinned around the empty stem of his pipe. Satisfied with the impact of his revelation, Cleve gestured for everyone to sit, and he launched into an account of his honorable defeat at the hands of this warrior, to whom he was wife.

"We even got a son," he said. "Back over at the camp, with my dog playing nursemaid. 'Course she done the most of that work, but you'd never know it. She never slowed down, and she tricked the fur raider that intended to kill us both.

"She'd have killed him if I hadn't come to and got him. Then she went off into the woods, and after a while she came back with our son, William Wolf Sings on the Mountain Bennett."

Fellmore spat into the fire, the stream of tobacco juice black against the flames. His grunt was one of great respect. Then he turned to gaze at Cleve.

"Fur raider?" His tone was interested, for all trappers knew of those who liked better to steal them than to trap for beaver and mink and muskrat and lynx. "You ever know his name?"

Cleve glanced at Second Son. She read people quickly, he knew. She nodded slightly, and he said, "Jules Terrebonne. He came after us to take the plews we had from Lavallette. Seems he'd been keeping watch on the old man, planning to rob him, just before we had our set-to and took off first.

"He came within next to nothin' of taking us out, and he would have, too, if Second Son hadn't fooled him into thinking she was about to give birth then and there.

When he bent over her, she grabbed him and was chok-
ing the life out of him when I came to and grabbed him
from behind.''

Pulliam sucked on the pipe stem, his gaze enigmatic.
"So what did you do? Which one kilt him?''

Cleve glanced again at his wife, sitting straight and yet
quite relaxed in this circle of alien men. He took a tin
cup of coffee from Fellmore and blew on it before
answering.

"Neither one, actually. We tied him to a tree, cut off
his clothes, and left him to freeze. He was a bad'un,
friends. I wouldn't have left him alive if he hadn't just
killed a good friend of mine.''

The group was silent for a while. The crackle of the
fire, the constant whine of the wind, the occasional
stamp or snort of a horse were the only sounds breaking
the quiet.

Then Second Son bent forward to pour the dregs of
her coffee onto the fire. "An evil man is made for death,''
she said, her tone that used in tale-telling around the
lodge at night. "He gave unjust and dishonorable death
to others, and in time he had so many stolen scalps, so
much innocent blood, so many curses from the dying
upon his spirit that they rose up and drowned him in
their flood.

"So it was with Terrebonne. I saved him, many seasons
ago when he was brought by a maddened horse into the
country of my people. He was almost frozen, and I took
him back to the village of my band and we fed him, even
in the Hunger Moon, and kept him warm in our lodges.

"When the weather warmed, he grew fat and began
talking of going back to his trapping in the mountains.
But before he went, he came to visit me in my lodge.
Though I was a warrior, I had no wife at that time, and I
was alone.'' She cast a mischievous glance toward Cleve.

In that moment she seemed totally feminine. "He would not believe that I was a man among my tribe, and he attempted to use me as a woman, against my will.

"When he left my fire, he was no longer a man, and his testicles roasted in the coals. This gave him a fine rage against me, which never cooled." Her face glowed serenely in the firelight, its expression unruffled.

There was a stunned silence among her listeners. The whistle of the wind echoed the intake of breath at the end of her tale.

Carson's mouth opened and closed again without emitting a sound. Pulliam took the pipe from his mouth and carefully stowed it in his empty tobacco pouch. Fellmore stared at Second Son, his face enigmatic, but Cleve could see in his eyes a gleam of approval.

He had the feeling that this was the time to rise and go, leaving the men to digest this information. It was likely that the tale would give them all they needed to know about his wife, and he felt certain not one of them would ever offer her any affront.

What others might do, when they reached the Rendezvous, there was no way of knowing, but Cleve smiled as they moved through the night toward the faint coals of their fire. Second Son did know how to give warning without giving offense, that was for sure and certain.

Snip came to greet them before returning to his watch over the infant. Cleve unrolled their bedding after covering over the fire, and Second Son brought Billy Wolf to lie between them. When they had quieted, and even Snip was asleep, he was still thinking of the things he had been told by Fellmore and his friends.

"Second Son?" he whispered, in case she had already fallen asleep.

"Ai?" she replied.

"I been wondering about the others I left Missouri

with—Prevot and Bridwell and the rest of Ashworth's bunch. They got through all right. Carson met up with the Shooner brothers last summer, and they told him about the orders they brought with them from the company, telling them how to find the get-together. I'd wondered how it got around so wide, with this country as wild and broke up as it is."

He heard her chuckle. "You have not noticed the peeled bark on the trees as we came? Until we left the direct route because of the Pawnee, there were marks pointing the way."

"I thought those were Indian sign," he said. Would he never become as quick as this Cheyenne? "They tell me he built mounds of dirt or piles of rock along the main routes in and painted the top rocks red so his men could find the way. That Ashworth's a smart man, and a fair one, too. I talked with him considerable, before he went back after the horses, and he seemed like somebody that would do what he set out to do."

She sighed. "It troubles me, Yellow Hair, to see so many white men in this country. The French were few, and they did not change the land. They took our ways and did not try to change them. But I now know you, and though you do not realize it, if you are like others of your kind, you will change a great many matters here on the plains and in the mountains before you are done."

Cleve said nothing more, but he was thinking about her words even after she drifted into sleep. He thought of his father's furious assault on the forest around his fields, as if the trees' very existence had been an affront to his control. Even in his short life along the Little Sac River, he had seen newcomers arrive and clear and plant and change the country until he hardly recognized it as the place to which they had first come.

He was badly afraid that she was right. Would his kind

spread over this wild country the way they had over the land east of the Big River and cut down the forest, plow the plains, making a tame and civilized place of it?

The thought made him shudder, but he was helpless to prevent it, he knew. His mother's teaching had given him glimpses into the ancient past. Reading her battered copy of Julius Caesar's *Gallic Wars,* he had seen the way the Romans bulled their way into other countries, over other people, and shaped the world to their own liking.

When he closed his eyes, he saw in his imagination those mounds pointing the way to this meeting of trappers. The red rocks atop the markers glowed in the sunlight of his mind, signaling a victory for the forces and pressures that seemed always to come from the east and roll over whatever lay in the lands of the setting sun.

chapter

— 10 —

It was with much relief that Prevot saw the line of peaks to the south, whitecapped and forbidding, rise from the high prairie along the Sketskedee. He had followed the sign left by Ashworth's men, and that had posed no problem for his group, but they had, after joining forces again, kept a wary eye on their backtrail. When you knew there was a threat at hand, you didn't relax for a minute.

But now they were nearing the fork that Ashworth had indicated as the rendezvous for his wide-flung bands of trappers. Already Emile could see distant plumes of smoke from campfires, as if a large number of others had already arrived.

He wondered, not for the first time, if this new venture

was workable and how many others outside the Ashworth enterprise might take the opportunity to trade
their furs here conveniently at hand instead of making
the long trek to the Hudson's Bay Company fort on the
Columbia River.

His heart beat more quickly at the thought of seeing
many old friends and new people, swapping tales, trading jokes and punches, and generally kicking up his
heels after these seasons of hard work. As they turned
toward the place of smokes he chuckled softly.

Levreaux, just behind him, chuckled, too, reading his
mind as he usually did. "We are not so ver' old, eh,
Emile?" he asked. He kicked his horse forward to ride
beside his friend. "We have the thirst for whiskey, the
need for *tabac*, the desire for wrestle with someone we do
not know and to pound his head into the ground, *n'est-ce
pas?*"

Prevot slapped Paul on the back, raising a cloud of
trail dust from his fringed buckskin shirt. "It seem as if
William have some few already there, *non?* I see four—
five—six smokes, even from so far. I taste the coffee . . .
ahhh, and the can peach, perhaps."

He waved Jim Bridwell forward, and the young man
trotted up, his grim face already lightening with anticipation. "You ride ahead, *mon ami*, and tell those fellow
we come, eh? We don' want them to think we sneak up
like hostiles, I think. Some will be nervous, perhaps, at
being so close to other who are unknown to them. Say
that Emile comes, yes? And then you have the drink for
me, until I arrive."

The boy was gone in a cloud of dust. Then Emile
settled into a steady pace as the mountains grew taller
and more forbidding, their white tops shining brilliantly
in the summer sun. Now he could see the painted tipis of
Indian villages scattered in random arcs over the plain.

Herds of horses grazed on the lush grass, so soon to be browned by drought and heat.

As his troop drew near he recognized the tipi decorations, which depicted buffalo hunts and raids for horses taking place beneath a large red circle denoting the sun, and he kicked his mount to a trot and yelled as he approached. "Sun Turns Red! My frien', how does your scalp attach itself, eh?"

The children who had been making rabbit snares in the shade of the tipi looked up, their small brown faces wary. Then one recognized Prevot, and she began to grin. There was a rapid chatter of Absaroka among the small ones, but they did not approach him. The door flap was filled with a large shape, and their grandfather emerged to look up at the Frenchman.

Sun Turns Red did not smile or raise his hand, but with a dignified inclination of his magnificent head he indicated that Prevot should join him inside the shelter, whose walls were turned back to allow the circulation of air. Despite the heat a small heap of coals flickered in the center of the space, and over it, hung from its tripod, a rabbit turned on a thong, the juices smelling delicious as they dripped onto the remnant of the fire.

Otter Woman, his oldest wife, ducked her head, smiling to see this longtime friend return to her lodge. She took down the rabbit, set it in a stone dish, and dismembered it swiftly.

"It is a strange thing," said Sun Turns Red, "that when there is food, I look up to see my friend Fox Head approach."

Prevot pushed back his foxhide cap and sighed. "It is a strange thing," he repeated, "that whenever I have the greatest hunger, my friend Sun Turns Red always appear with food ready for eating."

Both chuckled, that deep grunt of laughter, unaccom-

panied by a smile, that denoted humor. Then Emile
looked again at the dark necklace hanging from the neck
of his old friend. At first glance one might have thought
it was decorated with bear claws, but closer inspection
told the onlooker that those stiff pendants were human
forefingers. Between each of the stiff digits were quill
beads, dyed red and yellow, spaced with small bones
from the spines of rabbits and badgers.

"You take another one, I see," Prevot said. "I think
you are too wise now to go to battle, but you are too brave
to stay away from it, eh?"

"Even the old must be foolish, sometime," the old
man said. "The young, they think when the grandfather
becomes cautious, he has become afraid. One must
teach them better, from time to time. So I have raided a
Blackfoot village and have taken another decoration for
my necklace. That one needed it no longer."

Emile accepted the filled pipe that Otter Woman
offered, puffed it once, and passed it on to his old friend.
It was reassuring to find that this one never changed.
He pitied anyone who ever thought the old man to be
beyond defending his own people or attacking any threat.

He stared out through the open wall at the plain
visible between the adjacent tipis. The grassy stretch was
alive with horses, children, dogs. In the distance he
could see another scatter of shelters, the poles and flaps
of which were arranged a bit differently from those of
the Crow. Blackfoot, he was certain.

"You think that so many tribe, they will keep the peace
here all together?" he asked his old friend. "I see
the Pied Noir, and far beyond them a Pawnee camp.
There are ver' old grudges among these who come to
this trade place."

Sun Turns Red shifted slightly to look in the direction
of Emile's gaze. His expression did not change, but his

wrinkled eyelids crinkled a bit more deeply when he stared toward the distant assemblage of Blackfoot.

"These men who hold this trading have made laws. Any who breaks them must go and cannot exchange furs for weapons and tools. Any who bring old wars here and fight with another tribe can never return to any future rendezvous, they say. I think there will be no trouble. Not here." The black eyes turned toward Emile, and both men nodded.

The trail homeward might become exciting for some of those now camped so peacefully along the Sketskedee and the creek leading into it. Emile wondered about the group his people had met on their backtrail. There was never a good time to relax, here in the wild lands, and his return to his intended trapping country would be tense and suspicion filled.

"Who is here now? I see a pony paint with red and yellow hand and lightning bolt. Kill with the Lance have bring his young men? I do not know they trap for the *vair*. The Pawnee they hunt and they farm too far to the east."

"They bring very few beaver," said Sun Turns Red. "They have come, I think, from curiosity. Some have already traded fine robes for steel knives and iron pots, and I think they will think hard about furs before another winter passes."

"And there is tipi way over there beside the creek, just barely in range of these old eyes, that look like Running Dog's. Even the Hunkpapa are here! I am surprise that they come from so far." Emile squinted into the glare, but the figures painted onto the buffalo hide remained the same. It definitely belonged to Running Dog, who, if not a friend, was an honored enemy of his from the old days.

He dug into the rabbit and Otter Woman smiled to

see the relish with which he ate. When the last morsel was finished, she put another fat carcass on the tripod to cook for the children, and the two men moved out of the tipi into the shade.

The long string of his packhorses had passed and was now dwindling toward the confluence of the streams, where sheds had been erected to protect the trade goods. He sighed with satisfaction. This first of his ventures for Ashworth had gone well.

When he rode into the main camp, his companions had the horses unloaded and Bridwell was already flushed with whiskey as he supervised the location of their own campsite. He waved and yelled as he saw Emile approaching, and Prevot turned toward the spot chosen by his group.

"Have you anything lef' in the jug, *mon ami*?" Emile called to the younger man. "I send you to take drink, not to draw the well dry!"

Jim handed him the half-empty jug and led his horse away. Prevot turned the container up and took a modest swig, rolling the liquor around on his tongue. This was certainly not the best or even among the best he had ever tasted. Where was the fiery sensation at the back of the tongue and down the gullet to warm the stomach? Only a faint flicker of warmth followed the slug downward.

"He have water the booze," he said to Paul, who had come quietly up behind him. "Smart man, that Guillaume. He will make, I predict, as much money from the profit on the trade good as he will on the fur."

Levreaux snorted. "I have already see what he have with him. You are right. This will be the profitable venture. Just the bale I have look at riding through the rest of the camp will make Ashworth a ver' rich man. I like him, make no mistake, but I think he will not continue this long. He will sell out to some of those who look with greedy eye at what is to be made here.''

He led Emile to the casual shelter the two of them would share, at the edge of the spot they had chosen some distance from the main encampment. Bridwell had moved their party entirely through the enclave to the farther side, against the wood that straggled up the slopes of the foothills into the mountains to the south.

Here they were upstream from all the other groups, the water of the creek unpolluted by men and animals. There was shade for their shelters and grass, which, though less thick than that on the plain, would be ample for their horses. Emile grinned his approval as he followed Paul to their quarters.

"That Jim, he is the smart young fellow, *non?*" he said. "He have find the best of all the places for us, and we are ver' near the trading sheds *aussi*. Have he also put the coffeepot upon the fire and the stewpot on to boil?"

Levreaux grunted as he sank onto the bedroll under the shelter flap. "Not yet. I smell the rabbit on you, Emile. You have again visit your Absaroka friend when he have food ready on the fire. It is some sort of genius, I believe. We have not yet had food, though the trader, they pass out whiskey on the credit until we make the deal on our plew."

Emile turned toward the spot where William Shooner was fanning a flicker among the dried sticks piled haphazardly together. "*Mon dieu!* You have live for two winter out here and never have learn to make the fire properly? I am ashame of you!"

He knelt and rearranged the wood to form a conical shape over the small wood and tinder in which glimmers of sparks still shone. Then he bent and blew heartily until thin curls of blue smoke began to rise. As he settled back on his heels he looked up at the younger man.

"You have the *tristesse*, my frien'. Tonight, we will talk, yes? I have wonder about your brother, and I know you have the pain. When we have settle in, then you come to the shanty of Paul and me, and we will speak of old days together."

Shooner jerked his head in a half nod and turned away abruptly, heading for his own shelter. Emile watched him go, wondering how to comfort the boy for the loss of his brother. The rollicking pair had enlivened their journey up the Missouri, as well as later when they took to the horses and traveled overland. It was a shame . . . but this was harsh land, and death waited around every bend and over every hill.

Emile waited until most of the latecomers had found their campsites and checked in with the traders at the sheds before he went to see the setup for himself. He found himself impressed, for the trade goods were organized sensibly, located so they could be covered from rain if necessary and locked away in heavy chests, under guard, at night.

There was a very large complex of empty pole-sided shelters for the bales the company hoped to trade for as well. As he was walking around that group Prevot found himself face-to-face with a man he recalled with no enthusiasm whatever.

"Yoder," he said, with no warmth in his tone. "You are here, I see. With Terrebonne, I suppose?"

Ben Yoder stared at him, identified him in the dimming light, and leaned against a post that held up the shed roof. "Not so's you'd notice. He's done gone and got hisself lost, and that's a fact. Taken off back before winter more than set in good, and we haven't heard anythin' from him or Philippe since. I take it he's dead, so I'm the new boss of our bunch."

"Then I bid you good night," said Emile, brushing past the American and heading for his camp.

"Don't be so cocky, Frenchy!" Yoder called after him. "I may not be old Jules, but you're goin' to be surprised how smart I kin be when I put my mind to it."

"*Merveilleux!*" Emile said over his shoulder. But as he moved away he wondered just how effective a leader of cutthroats and thieves Ben Yoder might prove himself to be. If there was anything the mountains did not need, it was someone to take the place of Jules Terrebonne—if, indeed, that villain was actually dead.

He hurried toward the glimmer of the fire serving all the shelters of his party, feeling a shiver of apprehension travel down his spine. Yoder's gaze was following him through the darkness, he felt certain, chilly and speculative. Was it the group that villain led that his own had met at the head of that ravine back upriver? And did the burly American intend to relieve them of their trade goods as they returned to the mountain streams and another year of labor?

Paul Levreaux looked up from his seat on a chunk of wood. "Young Shooner, he wait for you in our shanty, Emile. I think he want to talk. I wait here for you, and if you need me, jus' call and I will come. That young man, he have great hurt, I think."

Emile smiled to himself as he went toward the shelter. He prided himself upon his toughness. He never showed pain or fear, even in the most terrible circumstances. The core of him, where his loyalties and his capacity for friendship lived, was carefully hidden and revealed only when someone he felt responsible for or to was in need. This was such a time.

He peered under the fly at the waiting boy, who was staring into the smudge of fire as if very far away. But William looked up as Emile ducked to enter.

"'Lo, Emile," he said, settling himself, cross-legged as the Indians did. "You sure you want to waste your night in talk? I see some tipis out there, and I'll bet there's some willing fillies somewhere among all that red meat."

It was tough talk, but Prevot knew it was bravado. This boy, hardly twenty even now, was in pain. It showed in his face and in every move he made.

"Tell me about the brother, *mon ami.* I know you have the need," he said, poking the ends of burned sticks into the smudge and kindling it to a blaze. "Vince, he was my friend as well as you, and I would like to know what happen to him. You have go north toward Colter's Hell, I think. What happen to you there?"

Shooner gulped audibly, but his control didn't falter. "We done it," he said. "Went up and down them side-winder mountains till we was tired and finally come out on a ridge above the damnedest valley I ever seen in all my life. There was a waterfall must've been hundreds of feet high on the other side, and in between was trees and grass full of buffalo and moose and elk and deer like a barnyard full of cattle. A man could live up there, iffen he didn't freeze to death in winter, and never want for nothin'."

He poked the fire with a stick and spat into the coals. "We found streams so full of beaver the little devils was steppin' on each other's toes, seemed like. Ponds full of lodges was like specks on a dog.

"Once it cooled down, we was set up fine, had a nice cabin built and the traps ready to go. You never seen so many plews as we taken that first winter. We never stirred a peg out of our tracks over the summer, because we didn't want nobody to find our spot by trackin' us back."

"You have bring a fine catch," Emile agreed. "Prime pelts, they all seem, though I have not examine them close in the bale."

"Well, the next winter was even better, but it must have been about midwinter—everything was froze as tight as a tick—when Vince come down with a cold. His head stopped up and he snorted and blowed and coughed till it was hard to sleep in the same house with him.

"I picked pine and fir needles and brewed up tea like Ma used to, and it seemed to help a little for a while. I made him stay inside when he got so he was dizzy all the time. But he began to cough like he was going to shake hisself apart.

"Sounded like there was water in his chest the way it gurgled when he tried to breathe." Shooner looked up, and the pain in his eyes told Emile how terrible his helplessness had seemed while his brother fought for life. Even with the ruddy light of the fire on his face, he looked pale and drawn.

"It was like he drowned, Emile. Struggled for a breath and then let it out like it hurt. Got slower and slower, and he quit even tryin' to eat. Just drunk water now and again or sucked snow. He went from the chucklehead you knowed to a little skinny fellow not much heavier than he was when we was boys. His bones poked out of his face, and his eyes they burnt holes in me when I looked at him.

"He talked a lot of nonsense, and then it was like he was little again, back home with Ma and Pa and the rest of us kids. It was almost like goin' home myself to hear him go on. Then one day he looked up at me and knowed me. By then he was nothin' but a skeleton, but he reached up one hand, real shaky and light as a feather, and taken mine.

"'Bill,' he said. 'You done a good job.' And then he let out his last breath, and that was it. I buried him in a snowdrift till the weather warmed. Then I dug him a

deep grave on a bluff under a bunch of little aspens and
I put a big chunk of rock at his head. He's got a nice view
up there, has Vince."

Emile said nothing. He didn't offer a comforting hand.
That wasn't the way with a mountain man. Instead he
pulled the rest of Bridwell's jug out of his possibles bag
and held it out. "You suck on this, *mon ami*. It will make
you feel better, *comprends?* An' then you go and get more
and kick up the heels with the other *jeunes hommes*.

"Have the *plaisir* twice, once for you, once for your
brother who cannot now be with us. You have done the
best you know, and no man can do more." He pushed
the boy's shoulder roughly. "And you don't think abut
anything but have the fun, *n'est-ce pas?*"

But when the retreating steps had gone out of hearing,
Emile sat and gazed into the fire almost as sadly as
Shooner had done. This was a terrible country in some
ways and a marvelous one in others. He wondered why
he loved it so and why, given the choice, he would never
return to New Orleans, even if he had still owned his
brothel there.

A heavier step approached up the hillside, and he
glanced up to see a familiar face peering under the flap.
"*Mon dieu!*" he said. "It is not the Joe Ferris! It is the
ghost, yes?"

Old Joe chuckled and sidled into the space where
Shooner had sat. "It's me all right," he said. "Got here
yestiddy and saw your bunch ride in, but I didn't spot you
with 'em. You must've stopped off to visit your Absaroka
friend.

"Soon as that youngster—Bridwell, is it?—told me you
was here, I come along to chew the fat. Been a while,
Emile."

Prevot nodded. "Maybe five year? We last met on the
Popo Agie, if I recall. You were just come back from St.

Louis and you had the big fellow work with you—Collis,
I think. He is here, too?"

Ferris shook his head sadly. "No, the Bloods got old
Collis, back in the mountains. I had to cut his throat,
'cause they left him pretty tore up, and dyin' of his
wounds would've been a hell of a lot worse than ending
it quick. But I've had a hard time of it since, thinking
about how I done took a man's life when he wasn't
aimin' to take mine first."

Prevot sighed, but he didn't let it show. For years he
had been something like the father confessor to any who
had troubles. First Shooner, now this red-faced preacher
needed solace. It was time to change the subject.

"I have see the pony of Kill with the Lance down there
in the grassland as we come through. You know that
one?" he asked.

"Do I know him? I lost a string of packhorses to him
once, back along the Cheyenne, and the son of a bitch
laughed as he rid off with 'em. I been keepin' him in
mind ever since. Yes, he's here, and he's lookin' for
somebody or something. I keep an eye on that red-
tail, and he's out for blood or my name ain't Old Joe
Ferris. But there's somebody worse here, and that's Jules
Terrebonne's sidekick, Ben Yoder."

"I have just see that one," said Emile. "He seem to like
it that he is now the *chef* of that band of thief. He say
Terrebonne disappear and have not been heard from.
Though that one is not to be depend on, even to stay
dead, I think."

"We got some really bad eggs here, and that's no joke.
Though I have to say that this Ashworth's done a good
job of keepin' the peace so far. His men set their rules,
and they've already sent a bunch of young Bloods skitin'
back north with their ears scorched by their old chiefs
for pickin' fights with other youngsters camped out

there on the plain. The older Injuns want to trade, and that's no joke."

"Good. Perhaps it will keep the peace. I have see many bad thing at the trade fort, Ferris, and it is in my mind that this need not be so dangerous for those who come. But now I have the thirst. You will come with me to draw against my credit for more liquor?"

The preacher shook his head sadly. "I oughtn't to. I know that. But I'm a weak man and a sinner and I want a drink something fierce. So I'll come, old friend, and you keep shakin' your finger at me to remind me I'm doin' wrong."

Laughing, Emile led the way down the hill toward the traders, whose dispensations of watered-down whiskey already had the camp echoing with gunshots, wild whoops of laughter, and yells of high spirits from those gathered there.

It was good to see Ferris again, though his religion was not Emile's and his prohibitions struck the Frenchman as crazy. But he was an old friend, and tonight they would get thoroughly drunk together and wipe out the sadness of the world for just a little while.

chapter

— 11 —

There hadn't been many people in his part of Missouri; as they rode into the encampment Cleve realized that he had never in his life seen so many folks all in one place. Indians of all sorts, Frenchmen, Spaniards, Americans from New England and Kentucky and just about everywhere else. He hadn't known there were so many white men spread through this wild and seemingly empty region.

His long time in the cleanliness of mountains and prairie had sensitized his nose to human smells. The wild clean scent of Second Son was now as familiar as his own, as was that (compounded of baby-smell, the often damp moss that formed his diaper, and whatever spit-up he had recently emitted) of his son.

Now he sniffed the air as if it rose from some rich stew. Sweat, of course, and less pleasant things were mixed with the stink of horses and the odors of the Indians, which ranged from dried grass, animal fat, and the stuff they used to paint their faces to the sharp scent of civet that some used to repel mosquitoes.

Few of the smells were pleasant, yet in the aggregate the effect was almost intoxicating. He wanted to ride ahead, yipping and yelling as some others seemed to be doing as they approached the trading camp from the other side of the grasslands.

His older companions, however, held their sober gait, and Cleve, feeling his youth as he had never done while dealing with mountains and grizzlies and people who wanted to kill him, repressed his impulses and followed beside Second Son. She was dressed again in her finest, the pale deerhide spotless, the red and yellow of the quill beadwork shining brilliantly in the sunlight.

He kept glancing sideways, marveling that this wild and impressive warrior was the mother of his child. Though she seemed perfectly relaxed, if one of the packhorses strained at his line or tried to balk, she was after it immediately. Her methods with horses, though not cruel, were highly effective, and seldom did the same horse balk twice.

He usually let her attend to such things. It was pure pleasure to see her kick Shadow into a lope, bend forward over the roached mane, and shape up the string again with perfect ease and no lost motion.

Shadow paced proudly now, among the tumult of the camp, as if she understood the need for show as they left the Indian encampments behind and wove their way through clusters of shelters of all kinds. From her rider's shoulder hung the cradleboard, and Billy Wolf's eyes shone from its top as brightly as his mother's beadwork.

Shadow's colt, Blaze, frisking behind his mother for most of the journey, seemed intimidated at being among so many men and horses. He now kept close to his dam's side, where Snip kept watch on his human baby and this small animal that seemed to have been added to his responsibilities.

Cleve grinned inside as he saw the curious glances following his wife. Warriors didn't ordinarily carry babies with them. This warrior seemed entirely too stern to approach with questions, however, so the various bearded and leather-clad trappers merely howdied and waved.

Fellmore, who seemed to know most of those assembled here, returned their greetings cheerfully, but he didn't stop until he found a spot to his liking. "You want to camp near us again?" he asked.

Cleve had talked about this with his wife the night before. "Let us go by ourselves," she said, when he asked her. "I know how to camp in a large village without having other people's dogs at our door or their children darting under the hooves of our horses. We will go up into the foothills, where the forest is."

"But that's so far from everything!" he had objected. "I want to talk to the other fellows, maybe get drunk. Pa never let me drink, back in Missouri, and I've never had a chance since. Looks as if a man has a right to find out how it feels. . . ."

He saw a strange look dawn in Second Son's eyes— almost the expression she sometimes had when she looked at Billy Wolf, as if she suddenly understood something she had not known before.

She'd smiled then. "You will go and talk and drink with the others, but the baby needs quiet. We will wait for you in the tipi we will build, once we find pines of the proper size. But let us not get too near these men. They are good men, I am sure, but we must have space about us if I am to be content.''

Now, following Shadow, Cleve saw that she was heading some distance beyond the last flimsy shelter, toward a spinney of alder high on the slope, set about with tallish pines. When she stopped and waited for him to catch up, he saw that this location would allow them to look down over the entire encampment. Those who came and those who went would be under their gaze, and if Kills with the Lance appeared, they would know.

"Good enough," he said. "Now I'd better go back and unload the packhorses before they get tired of standing hitched to the poles at the sheds. Ed said he'd watch them for us, but I don't want to be a bother to him.''

Feeling obscurely guilty, he turned back down the slope toward the place where his string waited, impatiently stamping and flicking flies away with their tails, amid a turmoil of talk and men and animals and the sharp stink of horse dung. When he arrived, Fellmore waved and went about his own business. Cleve waited until one of the tally men had time to count his bales and assess the skins.

It was a long process. Around him others were going through the same course, and when at last Cleve held in his hands the tallies for his plews, the sum represented there was larger than he had ever dreamed it might be. The combination of his and Second Son's efforts with Henri's seasons of work came to what seemed a fantastic sum.

He stopped at the whiskey barrel and dickered for a goodly supply of liquor, which the seller decanted into jugs, with the first of his profits. Fellmore had warned him that the stuff would likely be cut with water, as the trading forts did, so he bought six, just to be on the safe side.

There was a whole long counter full of whipsticks, flints, frizzens, gunstocks, skinning and fighting knives, gunpowder, lead bars, and bullet molds. He knew that this was the time to do his serious buying, before he got all heated up with excitement and whiskey and lost his ability to make a sharp bargain.

There was a box of metal arrowheads, shiny and sharp. He bought a bagful for Second Son, as well as himself. He still found the bow much faster and easier to use than the flintlock, in many situations. Further along, he found iron cooking utensils, and he bought a coffeepot to replace the leaky one they had salvaged from Henri's goods.

There were fine woolen blankets and shirts, boots, which he ignored for he had found the moccasin more comfortable, and sewing kits with real steel needles, along with tough thread. He bought several of those, knowing that Second Son would learn quickly to use them, once he showed her how.

Coffee, beans, dried fruit, flour, the food stock seemed boundless, after his years of making do on what he could scrounge from the countryside. He stocked up with a lot of that, and then he found that his purchases were going to be more than he could carry. He moved clear of the throng and stared uphill, trying to see his own camp, but it was too well hidden.

Then he grinned mischievously and whistled his old signal to Socks to come running. High above there was a whinny and the alders shook. Then he saw his horse heading down the slope, avoiding fires, people, and shelters with the grace of a dancer. Good old Socks!

When the animal's soft nose pushed moistly into his neck, Cleve patted his jaw and turned back to the sheds.

The trader who had dealt with him stared in astonishment as he returned to begin loading his supplies.

"Some horse you got there," the man said. "What you take for him?"

"You could trade this entire camp and throw in Missouri and it still wouldn't buy him," Cleve said. "He's saved my life at least once and come close a lot more times than that. No, there's no way I'd sell Socks." He turned to survey the next display.

"You got a lot of doodads there. I'll bring my wife down tomorrow to look at those; I don't know what she'd like. I don't see much woman-stuff, but she doesn't like that kind of thing anyway."

They went through the tally, deducting the purchases from the balance, and then Cleve led his burdened horse back toward his camp. There, Second Son had the frame of the tipi up, the freshly cut lodgepoles filling the air with their aromatic scent of resin. He hurried to help her lace the buffalo hides onto the frame, leaving the sides hitched up to let the breeze flow through.

A freshly skinned woodchuck hung from the stub of a branch, and before the afternoon was over, they had their own fire going just outside the door hole, the smell of the roasting meat enriching the air over a wide radius. Billy Wolf crawled about on a big skin that his mother kept specially for such exercise, and Snip lay dreaming into the fire, his gray whiskers twitching.

Cleve wondered why, with such richness here, he wanted so desperately to join the raucous crowd lower down the slope as they drank and shot off their guns and yelled in sheer exuberance. As he finished his last bite of meat he looked up to find Second Son's gaze meeting his.

"Now you go. Take your whiskey and your gun, for I see that the others have theirs. I will walk up the mountain with the baby and Snip, and we will look down over this new country and see what it is like. We will be asleep when you return, so do not hurry. White men are strange and have their own ways. Go and be a white man, Yellow Hair." She reached to touch his shoulder gently.

"But do not forget to return and become a Tsistsistas again." She turned away and picked up Billy Wolf and busied herself with tickling him.

Cleve felt a huge grin growing inside him. By God, he was about to become a real man at last. He'd heard the tales of the older men as they made their way along the Missouri, back when Ashworth's bunch first set out. He'd thought that doing such scandalous and exciting things as they bragged about would mark some magical turning point that would prove him a man among men.

He moved down the slope to the edge of the camp, maneuvered his way by the lights of the fires kindled outside shanties, canvas flaps, and even rude tipis, and found himself at last among the carousers. Lee Pulliam's was the first familiar face he saw, and he waved, a shout being inaudible in the din, and gestured toward a cluster of men swapping drinks and lies.

They slipped in among them and handed their own jugs around the rough circle. Cleve felt the first impact of the liquor go down his gullet like fire, even watered down as it was, and he realized that his lack of experience with the hard stuff was going to work to his disadvantage. Better to get really drunk so it wouldn't hurt so much.

He slipped away from the throng and found a quiet spot behind one of the sheds. The guard inside peered out at him suspiciously as he settled, but his purpose was obvious, so the man ignored him. Cleve tilted another jug to his lips and let the liquid gurgle down again.

This time, perhaps because the first had cauterized his

throat, it wasn't so bad. Tasted god-awful, of course, but that had been what he expected from the first.

How long he sat there he didn't recall afterward, but when he stood at last, the world slipped sideways, whirled for a moment, and then steadied, somewhat off kilter. Was this being drunk? He really saw nothing so great about it, though he did need to piss in the worst way.

He bumped into six men and the rear end of a horse before he got clear of the crowd and found himself within range of an unoccupied spot. He let fly, only to hear a roar of rage from someone who had evidently been taking a nap under the bush he honored with his stream.

"*Espèce de cochon!*" came the anguished yell. "I will take the head between these hands and twist it from the body!"

"If there isn't four of you," Cleve yelled back, "you better be ready for the damnedest fight you ever got into!"

In the flicker of the distant firelight a square shape heaved upward, making the bush quiver, and hurtled toward him, its flight somewhat erratic but true enough to bring the attacker within range of Cleve's fist. His knuckles met flesh with a wet *splop* and he dodged aside as the man tried to wrap him in a bear hug.

His feet, ordinarily so steady and dependable, seemed to have developed a will of their own. His dodge turned into a stumble, which developed into a full-fledged fall. He went down on hands and knees amid prickly duff and tried to push himself upright again with one heave.

That didn't work, either; his balance was so far off that he fell sideways and rolled just in time to keep from getting kicked in the face. The next time the foot swung, a dark blur in the night, he grabbed it with both hands and twisted with all his strength.

The man went down like an oak tree, with a heavy thud and a string of curses, which, being in French, did not add to Cleve's vocabulary of cusswords. While his opponent was thrashing and muttering Cleve took the opportunity to rise again, using a nearby sapling as a handy method for hauling himself upright.

The big fellow groaned and came up again, moving like a grizzly bear, crouched and ready, though still weaving with drink. Cleve saw, for a moment, two of him, then four, and he wondered for a panicky instant if his foe had taken him at his word and called in several allies. Then his vision steadied somewhat, and it was only a single man who seemed ready to rip his head from his shoulders.

Cleve ducked and lunged, butting the trapper in mid-belly. Again they went down, together this time, in an untidy heap. Floundering over and over in the bushes, poked with thorns and broken twigs, Cleve wondered for a split second if being grown and drunk and in a fight was really as much fun as he'd been led to believe. Then a fist connected with the side of his head, and the world blurred.

That gave the other man a chance to rise again. This time he kicked Cleve in the ribs, then dived on top of him and began pounding his head into the dirt. Since Cleve had left his head covering behind at the tipi with Second Son, his ears quickly filled with pine straw, dirt, and dead grass, and occasional sharp pebbles proved to be mightily painful to his cheekbones and skull.

With a desperate heave he unseated his opponent and rolled away, panting and cursing. His head had begun to ache, and both his eyes seemed to be trying to see out of the same socket, which gave the flickering space about him a strange and unsteady look. He felt certain that this was not the game he had anticipated when he came down the hill.

Then there was no time for thinking, for his foe was again diving at him, this time getting those formidable arms around him and hugging him so tightly he couldn't breathe. Cleve brought up his knee and felt it sink into the bastard's groin.

There came a sharp gasp—*"Merde!"*—and the arms loosed just enough to let Cleve expand his lungs, widening his shoulders to free them, and get away again. This time, despite his dizziness, he spun on his toes and flung a wild fist directly into the shadowy face. At the same moment another fist came out of nowhere and busted him fully between the eyes.

With a sigh half of pain and half of relief, Cleve fell backward amid the brush and all the lights went out.

His mouth tasted as if a cat had used it. Cleve moved, tried to turn aside to spit, but instead a gush of sour liquid poured out of him. When he stopped retching, he tried opening his eyes, but it was even darker than it had been when the fight began. Only sparks of light from the few remaining campfires touched the bruised leaves hanging just above his eyes.

"Ugh!" He got an elbow under him, then his hands, and pushed himself up to sit amid the tangle where he had fallen.

The night spun around his head, and he held on to the ground with both hands to keep from falling up into the treetops. Again he vomited, bending forward so the spew would go between his knees onto the ground.

A moan from nearby made him wipe his mouth hastily and try to locate its source. If that big bastard came at him again and he was still able to run, he intended to leave like a shot.

The bushes rustled loudly, and a dark shape sat up beyond the one beside Cleve. "*Merde!* I am get too old for such game, *non?*" someone muttered.

Cleve had slept out some of his drunk and thrown up more. Now his ears, no longer buzzing with liquor, recognized that voice.

"Emile?" he asked. "Emile Prevot, is that you there in the dark?"

"And who is it that want to know this?" came the suspicious question from beyond the bush. "I have many enemy, and I do not give my name to the chance comer in the night, *comprends?*"

"Cleve! Cleve Bennett, that you called Bear Ax, back at that winter fort on the Missou'. Don't tell me you've forgot me!" For some reason the thought that his mentor might have forgotten him was disturbing.

There was a moment of silence. Cleve assumed that the Frenchman was reassembling his wits in somewhat the painful fashion he had used for himself. Then the bushes shook again and the fellow stumbled to his feet.

"These drink, she warm the heart but she leave it ver' cold when she go, *non?* Cleve Bennett, that the Arickara kill, we think. This is a most strange meeting, my friend. Come to the fire. I think these reunion deserve a drink, *n'est-ce pas?*"

Cleve almost vomited again, thinking about putting even watered whiskey into his tenderized belly. Then he managed to stand.

"If you got coffee, I'll go. I need something to settle me down, I think. Haven't had a chance to drink in a long time now, and it's bothering me." Cleve decided it was time he got his lying sharpened up, too, as this was obviously a large part of any conversation he had overheard while getting drunk.

Prevot snorted, spat, groaned, and wavered through

the bushes with the noise of a stampeding buffalo. Cleve followed, not knowing where he was going, but he couldn't have found his own tipi anyway. Not until he was a lot soberer than he was now.

The Frenchman seemed to have the instinct of a hawk, however, for he wove his way through the disorganized jumble of habitations to the very edge, upstream, where a neat encampment showed that the discipline of the old group had not entirely disappeared. A big fire boomed in the middle of the arc of shelters.

Around it sat a number of men whose clothing was not what Cleve remembered but whose voices brought back acutely the long sessions of talk before the fireplace that first winter on the river. The faces in the firelight were older, seamed where they had been smooth, bearded where the first boyish fuzz had shown before, but they, too, were familiar.

Cleve felt suddenly embarrassed at his beardless condition. His father and grandfather before him had scanty beards, and it had been no problem to pluck out the hairs as they appeared. Second Son had made her disapproval of hairy-faced men pretty obvious during their first months together, when he had thought to grow a brushy one to keep his face warm.

But he beamed down at the upturned faces, now startled as if a ghost had appeared among them. Even his queasy stomach and fouled mouth couldn't ruin this moment.

"By damn, it's Bare-Ass Bennett!" That was Jim Bridwell, older and tougher and meaner but still recognizable, though the devilish glint in his eyes had been subdued to the faintest of twinkles.

"Sure is, Jim," Cleve said, taking the extended hand and dropping to sit between Bridwell and William Shooner. "Been a long time."

Shooner held out a jug, but Cleve shook his head. "Rather have coffee, if there's any in that pot."

A tin cup was sloshed full and reckless amounts of sugar added. When it was passed to him, Cleve held it for a moment between his hands, smelling the aroma of real coffee. It had been a while since Henri's hoarded bit ran out, and he had missed it desperately.

"I bet this stuff is high-priced," he said, rolling the first bittersweet sip around his tongue. "We seldom got any even when I lived back home in Missouri. Bringing it from the Coast all the way out here must cost a pretty penny."

"Drink up!" Prevot said from his place beyond the fire. "We are all rich tonight. In a while, perhaps, we will again be poor trappers, going away through the mountain to work ourselves thin, but for now we have money. And for what is that if not to share with friends?" He held up his jug and took a huge gulp.

Cleve shuddered, remembering the sensation in his unready stomach. The smell of the stuff was about to make him throw up, but he held out his cup with bravado. "Slosh a little in that, will you, Emile? I need some hair of the dog."

Mixed with coffee, it went down easier, and he began feeling more human and less like a dead buffalo left out in the weather to rot. He turned to Bridwell. "You look older, Jim. How'd it go with you the past couple of years?"

"The hell with me," the trapper said. "Tell us about you. You disappeared like you dropped off the edge of the world, and here you come poppin' up by the fire, big as life, without so much as a tall tale to tell about it. Here, you stretch out your legs, get comfortable, and tell us what in hell happened to you out there by the Arickara villages."

Cleve sighed. He didn't really feel like spinning a tale, but he owed these fellows some account of his years away from them. They'd been good friends, and while he no longer felt himself a part of the Ashworth venture, he did feel a strong bond of comradeship with this original group.

So he told the long tale of his escape, his flight and the hand-to-hand combat with his pursuer. They sat up when he mentioned his seasons with the Cheyenne. For some reason he made no mention of his wife and his son, but he gave a fairly accurate account of his time with Henri Lavallette.

"That Frenchy, he went plumb crazy, seems as if, and it ended up with him dead and us . . . me . . . taking off with all his plews. So don't think I murdered him for his stuff. He deserved to die, and he did. You know him, Emile?"

Prevot spat a stream of whiskey into the fire, making the blaze shoot up and sparks fly out in all directions. "I know that one. He is—or was—a good *associé*. I trap with him for three season, many year ago, but we part when he lose his temper and try to kill me with the knife.

"Henri, when he was *de bon humeur*, was good. When he reach the point of anger or when he desire what you have, then he was of the utmost evil. So I know what you say. He want something you have, *non*? And you must fight to keep him from take it?"

Cleve nodded, feeling a vast relief. He had been worried, deep down, that his peers might think him a thief and a murderer, but it seemed that he had a good advocate in this highly respected member of Ashworth's band.

He turned to Bridwell. "Now you, Jim," he said. "I want to know how you been doing since I took off across the plain, naked as a jaybird."

Obviously these men had been swapping tales, for the others settled with their jugs and their cups, waiting. Bridwell stared about, his face grim, even in the red light.

"You won't feel so fine and comfortable once I git done," he said. "But you asked, so here it is."

Cleve sipped his coffee and leaned back against an aspen bole. This was what he had wanted when he left his camp, not some anonymous fight in the bushes.

As Jim began his story the noisy camp below faded and the country that Bridwell began describing appeared behind Cleve's eyes, for he had seen places much like that on his own lone venture into the wild.

chapter

— 12 —

Although he had seen Indians steal the Ashworth expedition's horses and later had taken part in their ambush and siege below the Arickara villages, Jim Bridwell had, with the innocence of youth, felt that nobody he knew could possibly die. Of course he'd lost his grandmother a few years back, and later his grandfather, but they were old. Old folks died, everyone knew.

When the military relieved the embattled trappers after their skirmish on the Missouri, they had counted noses carefully. The band had lost one killed, four wounded, and a single man who could not be found at all. Cleve Bennett had been a special friend, and Jim was furious

that fate had taken him without leaving any sign of what
happened to him.

Before they reorganized and started off on horseback, instead of following the river, Bridwell questioned
the warriors he could find very carefully. He found an
Arickara carrying the brand-new Hawken issued to
Cleve, who had carved his initials into the stock. When
he saw that scrolled *CB*, young Jim almost lost his cool
temper.

Instead, however, he traded the Indian for the weapon,
using some of his carefully hoarded supply of sugar to
complete the swap. He'd carried that rifle himself, keeping the one the company issued to him for a spare,
through the years since. It had gone with him across the
Rockies and served him well.

Preferring to go his own way, Bridwell parted from the
company of Ashworth and Prevot near the Bighorn
River and set out into the mountains. And there his life
as a mountain man really began.

"I found me a nice little river, jumping alive with
beaver, and there I set traps that first winter. Caught me
a mess of 'em, too, and skinned them out as neat as could
be. I got lonesome, I guess, but there was so much to see
that even after it got too cold to trap, I just wandered
around lookin' at the sights."

He could still see those splendors behind his eyes, and
he strained to put into words the marvels he had seen.
"There was a waterfall at one end of a little valley, come
down over solid rock, but it'd cut a slot like you'd taken
a knife and sliced it out neat, where the water flowed.
One morning after a real cold snap I went up there just
to see if it was froze, and sure as God made little apples,
it was solid.

"It was like a whole bunch of swords made out of glass,
sharp icicles hanging straight down and little spatters on
the rocks to the sides, humped up like marbles, and big

swatches like lace where the splashes turned to ice while they was splashin'.

"The trees leanin' over the falls was covered with froze mist, all over, above and below, and they looked like the ghosts of trees. The sun was dancing over it all, making everything sparkle and shine, and the colors"—he still marveled at those—"they was better than rainbows, and I seen my share of those, too."

Emile Prevot smiled. "I have know those rainbows, up there in the mountain where the air is like the crystal. And I have seen the waterfall *gelé*—what you call frozen, too. *C'est merveilleux.*"

Bridwell sighed. Then he tried to look tough, for he was, after all, a hardened man of the woods, not a callow youth sighing over something too beautiful to put into words.

"The next spring I hid all them bales of plews and went wanderin'. There's mountains after mountains in this Rocky Mountain chain, boys, and I crossed 'em all. Some was dry and brown, those to the east of the range, and some on the west side was wetter with nice forests of pines and alders. Streams run down them west slopes and it's pretty green there.

"I come over a ridge about midsummer and there below me, beyond a few more ridges and peaks, was a sea. A real damn *sea*. I made certain I kept my directions right, and when I come out on the downward slope, the thing stretched out from side to side as far as I could see. On the other side was some brown mountains, way off in the distance, but I never seen no lake as big as that anywhere.

"Once I got down to it, I found out it's just as salty as any sea as well. I set a stick in the edge to mark if it had a tide, and when I went back the next day, it was all iced up with salt till it looked like it had froze, too. Like glass, it was. But that damn water's no good to man or beast. You got to go up one of the cricks running into it to get a drink.''

He leaned back against a tree and stared into the flames. ''But it wasn't all fun an' games, you'd better make book on that. I got caught by some Injuns. . . . Shoshonni got me fair and square, and if I hadn't been dumb enough to go swimmin' in that salty lake, they'd have got all my gear, too.

''But I'd hid my camp so they couldn't see it easy, and I give 'em so much trouble, bein' wet and slippery and bare as a fish, they just wrapped me up in thongs and jerked me along with 'em, instead of searching real good. I got dragged through every thornbush and burr patch for miles, running barefoot behind a big roan stallion that kept shittin' in my face.''

There came a roar of laughter, and Cleve passed him the jug that Bill Shooner handed to him. The warm gulp oiled his flow of words.

''They stopped in a ravine where there was a bunch of tipis and a whole passel of horses. I'd been pulled flat, draggin' through the brush and over the rocks, and I was skinless as a skunt rabbit by the time I slid up in a fresh pile of manure and come to a halt.

''It was a while before I knowed where I was, after that, though I recall being lifted and carried by somebody that didn't care that they dropped me a couple of times. But finally they set me down on the ground, and I laid there and passed out total for a long time.

''When I woke up, I was glued to the ground by my own blood, and somebody was steppin' in my face. The bastards had put me right where one of the squaws had to step over me to get in and out of her tipi. She got tired of steppin' high, I guess, and put her foot right on my nose.''

He raised a finger and pushed his long, thin nose, which moved to one side and remained there when he let it go. "Broke the damn thing, and it never has healed proper. Bled like a stuck hog, believe me, for a long time more, and when I was done, I swear I was bleeding pink instead of red.

"Once the fat old warrior that seemed to own me found out I was awake, he kicked me till I got up and then he shoved me over to one side so the squaw could go about her business easier. I guess I was in and out for a couple of days before I really knowed anything again, and by then I was one big mess of dry blood and shit and flies and scabs and I felt like I'd been drug backward through hell."

"The Indian, they are not tender of the captive," Prevot agreed. "I have been there myself, *mon ami,* and it is not the thing one recall with pleasure."

"Anyway, once I come to good, that squaw pushed me ahead of her down to a little crick and scrubbed me down with sand and handfuls of reed till I bled all over again. But she got the pus out of the infected cuts and scratches, and she rubbed me down with grease that stunk to high heaven.

"I don't know what she put in that stuff, but it must have been the real goods, because I never had no more trouble with the sores. There ain't even a scar, except the long one down my belly where I must've been drug over a stob or a sharp rock."

Shooner looked grim. "I wish I'd've had her with us," he said. "I lost my brother because I didn't know enough about curin' sick folks. Maybe the squaw could've saved him."

Cleve had been listening intently, but now he put his hand on Bridwell's shoulder. "But why did they keep you alive? If they didn't do anything to help you, I'd have thought they were going to have a high old time torturing you to death."

"That come down the pike some later," said Bridwell. "No, old Turtle Hat lost a son to the Blackfoot in the winter, and he wanted another. So they taken me in and let me find out if I was going to live or die before they did much of anything.

"Yellow Bird, the oldest of Turtle Hat's wives, tried to put a knife in me a couple of times, they told me later, because the son that was lost was hers and she didn't want no outsider takin' his place. But Little Fox and Singing Bear, the other two, was young enough and softhearted enough to keep dribblin' water in my mouth and feeding me a bit of broth from time to time. They're the reason I'm still alive."

He closed his eyes, reliving that time with no pleasure whatsoever. When he opened them again, he went on: "I carried wood and skinned game and scraped hides till I thought my fingers would come off. It's no joke to be an Injun, I tell you. I thought my ma worked hard, but at least she had a well outside the backdoor and a house that you didn't have to build every night before you could cook supper and go to bed.

"Them Shoshonni was movin' around after buffalo and elk and moose, and every day we was someplace we hadn't been the night before. And I was the handyman, woodcutter, and gen'ral whippin' boy of the whole entire camp. Got so I hated to see anybody coming at me, because I knowed they was going to take a whack at me as they passed."

"Why didn't you slide off into the bushes and take off?" Cleve asked. "I was sure lucky to get taken by the Tsistsistas. They were mighty good to me."

"I been with the Cheyenne a bit, too," Bridwell agreed. "But the bunch that got me was mad at the world, seemed like, and they taken it all out on me. By the time my feet was healed enough to do any travelin', we was so far from where I was took that I knowed I had to be smart or I'd never live to get back.

"I rocked along, keepin' my head down and saying nothin', though I learned enough of their lingo—sort of like what the Utes talk—to know what was going on. But I played dumb and never let on. They got so they'd talk about anything at all right there in front of me, so when they met a bunch more kinfolks, up in the edge of the mountains where the water is cold and the sun is hot, they never thought about warning me what was going to happen."

Bridwell reached for the jug again and gave it a long pull. He could still feel the chill in his gut he had felt the day he heard Turtle Hat dickering with another old bastard over the price for a white slave. It still turned his stomach to think what might have happened if he hadn't hidden his understanding of the Shoshonni tongue.

"The old man decided I was worth a paint pony and a wore-out mare, when one of the warriors in the other camp come over to bargain. That one said they needed some entertainment for the womenfolk . . . they hadn't had nobody to touch up with fire and knives for a long old while, and everybody's wife or sister or mother was gettin' edgy and snappish. It was about time to get their minds off tormenting their menfolk.

"So they made the bargain, and I kept right on working the skin they'd give me to soften, not letting on I knowed anything was in the wind. By then my feet was a lot better, and I'd been soaking them in every cold stream we come to, as well as making me moccasins out of scraps off the hides I worked.

"They'd give me a wore-out buffalo robe and a tattered deerhide shirt and leggin's, so the brush wouldn't cut me to flinders. I watched real close that afternoon, waitin' my chance, and after a while Yellow Bird sent me to the crick for water. I taken the clay pot and headed out, but she never seen me nor her pot again.

"Once I got out of sight along the crick, I filled that pot and tied it into a sling I made out of thongs I'd stole and hid by tyin' 'em around my waist. It was awkward, but I knowed there was some dry country I had to cross to get back to that sea where they catched me. It would be a lot easier with water than without.

"I taken off up that crick, keeping in water at least hip-deep and tryin' to step on nothin' but rocks, which there was plenty of. It went zigzagging up a hogback ridge, and by the time it disappeared into a hole, there was enough rock to hide the tracks of a whole passel of runaways."

Emile chuckled. "You learn ver' fast how to hide the trail when you run from the Indian."

"You're damn right," Jim said. "I didn't go back south the way they might expect me to, either. No, I went right up that ridge and over the other side, makin' certain sure I left no track behind me. That's a lot easier on foot than mounted, which was the only good thing about that.

"There's more ups and downs in that country than you can shake a stick at, and I upped and downed 'em all, I think. I headed south along the mountain chain, keepin' to trees and gullies as well as I could. There didn't seem to be anybody on my trail, 'cause I climbed up rocks and such late in the evening when there'd be campfires built, and never did I see a spark.

"Wasn't no horses moving in the open, either, any-time I watched, so I figured I had it made good. And then, just when I was gettin' set to turn back through a pass I found and go down toward that salt sea, where I might catch my horses and sure would find my plunder, I run right smack dab into a bunch of Blackfoot. What they was doing so far to the west I dunno, but I set down to rest in a cranny in the rock, and when I stood up, there they was, lookin' down at me like I was just what they wanted to see all their lives.

"I jumped like a jackrabbit, I tell you, and was gone down the ravine I'd been settin' in faster than any child you ever seen in all your life. They hadn't time to kick their heels into their horses till I was *gone*.

"Once I got out of sight good, I clumb out of the cut and taken off across a meadow of high grass. At the other side there was a spring, and I went down it like a trout, scooting on my butt or rolling along like some silly otter. Leaving no track, you better be sure. I never went noplace so fast, and there was no way them Blackfoot could have tracked me even if they'd knowed where I went.

"I come out in a little cup of a valley on the side of a mountain, and it was just plumb the peacefulest place I ever seen. There was a beaver pond in the middle, and four or five lodges, and the birch and alder and willow around the edge was all bein' chawed off for winter grub.

"I mighty near kilt me a beaver with my knife, but somehow I couldn't do it, once I thought about it. It wasn't like trapping. They was so easy and busy, and I just set and watched for a long time. Then I had a cold feeling in my innards that somebody was comin' over the ridge behind me, and it wasn't going to be no friend.

"I guess the longer you stay out here, the better your hunches get. I slid off into that pond without even a ripple, and I sunk down under and swum hard as I was able toward the nearest beaver lodge.

"That water was *cold*. But I kept my head under and

held my breath till my lungs near burst, and I found the entry hole about two seconds before I drowned. I shot through that bastard like a cannonball through a cannon, and when I come up, I was in a low, dim-lit place that smelled like wet beaver.

"There was a sort of ledge around the edges, and I could see eyes shining in the light that came through the chinks in the top of the lodge. Maybe eight beaver was resting there, and some little bitty ones was with 'em. They didn't even make a noise, just stared at me as if they wondered what sort of hairless beaver had took up room in their pool.

"On one side the ledge was just a sort of rim, and I moved over there and tried to see out. It was late afternoon, and the sun was lighting up the slope that rose to the top of the ridge. I poked a finger real careful into the thatch, and when I moved enough twigs and brush to one side, I could see a line of warriors sittin' on their horses while they drank out of the pond.

"I hadn't had time to think, so far, and now I tried my best to see if this was Shoshonni or them damn Blackfoot that had come so near catching me. Sure as hell, it was Blackfoot, and I'd have bet it was the ones I'd got away from before, but they didn't seem anxious or excited like they was on anybody's trail. They was just taking their ease, getting ready . . . by golly, they was about to camp for the night!

"I shivered like a wet dog. I was already cold and soaked and tired to death, and now I had to spend the night up to my neck in water in a beaver lodge. Sometimes it just don't seem fair, somehow."

Emile extended the jug again. "Life, she is not fair, ever. That is why God invent the whiskey."

Jim had to agree as the warm draft went down again.

"Well, I decided that it wasn't any worse to get bit to death by a beaver than to die of chill in the water, so I wiggled till I got my arms and legs workin' again and then moved over to the lowest part of the lodge and tried to climb up on it.

"Them crazy beaver didn't seem to care. I got up on the mud and sticks, and it felt as good as any feather bed I ever slept in back east. But it was still cold, for the sun was down. So I kept scroochin' closer and closer to the nearest beaver, which wasn't hard because we was pretty well crowded in there.

"Before you knowed it, I was snuggled in between a couple of 'em, snug as could be. A beaver, when you come right down to it, is *warm*. That fur coat keeps him cozy as a chestnut in a fire.

"We slept right well, all together there, though them little 'uns wiggled a lot. Even the mud ledge got warm enough so it didn't chill me off. It made me mighty glad I hadn't killed that critter by the pond. I didn't know if one of these was him, but it made no difference.

"They was helpin' me out, and I'd never trap there, no matter what. I hope nobody finds 'em. It's such a little pond, with only a handful of lodges, so that's not very likely, anyway."

He chuckled. "When they begun stirring around the next morning, I peeped through another hole in the lodge and the Injuns was gettin' ready to go, too. So I dived out through the underwater hole, and when I got ashore, I shaken for a while. Pretty soon the sun come up and I went off again, down toward that long valley where the sea is.

"And when I got there, which taken a long time and sore feet, my stuff was right where I left it. It taken me a week to find my horses and catch 'em and tame 'em down again, and by then it was gettin' on for fall, so I went back over the mountains and into the Swans. Somehow I'd lost my taste for runnin' into Shoshonni.''

Cleve leaned over and pounded his back. "That's a better tale than mine, by a long shot. Who'd've thought about hiding in a beaver lodge? It's for damn sure the Injuns never thought about anybody being there.''

A volley of shots from below the camp made all their heads turn. Emile grunted and put another piece of wood on the fire. "We are all here together, eh? Safe, for the time, and with friend. It is a good time, *n'est-ce pas*? But I have grow old, me, and I must have the rest. You young ones go on with the talk. I must find my blanket and close the eyes.''

To Jim's surprise Cleve rose, too. "I most forgot. I've a wife and son up there in the trees, and it's time I got back. If I can make it, that is.'' He extended his arms for balance and carefully set one foot before the other, wavering a bit but moving more or less in the direction he seemed to have chosen.

At the edge of the firelight he turned and waggled a hand. "See you later, Jim. You got—hic!—to meet my partner.'' Then he was gone.

Jim wondered what sort of Indian Cleve had married. Probably a Cheyenne girl, one of those tightly disciplined wenches he had tried to inveigle into his bedroll back in the prairie country, with notable lack of success.

He wondered what it would be like to have that sort of wife. But he knew his ma would skin him alive if he ever told her he'd meddled with a red-tail wench, no matter what the circumstances. You didn't marry a Cheyenne and then just leave, either. Not if you didn't want to wake up with a knife in your belly.

A huge belch sounded beside him, and William Shooner curled up on his side on the ground and began to snore. Jim looked across the coals at the other men's flushed faces. Their eyes were bleary with drink and weariness.

He yawned, grunted a muffled good-night, and lay flat, staring up into the stars until sleep closed his eyes. It was pure luxury not to have to keep watch.

chapter

— 13 —

Second Son was used to large gatherings of people when her tribe met on the plains for the summer buffalo hunts. She had seen as many tipis scattered about the country as now straggled over the grassland beyond the river, but these lodges were not those of her own people.

The other shelters, some neat, most haphazard, that the white men had put up roused contempt in her orderly soul. Their loud voices and random gunfire seemed unnecessary to her, and as soon as Cleve had gone down the slope and out of sight, she took her son and headed for the quiet reaches of the hilltop forest, which cloaked the slopes that formed the insteps of the mountains to the south.

Snip, of course, scouted out the way. Naturally, she went armed, for without bow and knife she never felt completely dressed. In strange country it was best to prepare for anything, and as she went upward she kept turning to stare down at the prairie land that now opened to her view.

She could see, even from such a distance, the markings and decorations painted on the buffalo-hide walls of the tipis and even some that had been daubed onto horses and shields. Crow were there, camped at a good distance from the Piegans and the Bloods. She detected the shape of Pawnee shelters, almost out of sight beyond a clump of trees.

That roused her curiosity. The Pawnee had, until rather recently, been farmers, grubbing in the dirt and living in lodges made of mud and poles. Her father had told tales of her people's first forays into the grasslands, and she knew that this place was very far afield for those fierce warriors to range.

Was Kills with the Lance down there, his hunting band mingling even now with the rest of this mixed group that had come to trade with the white men? She had a feeling in her gut that this was so, and if it were true, then she and Yellow Hair must be very careful.

Lance was proud, resentful of those who outsmarted him, and he would find a way to avenge himself upon the two of them, if he was given a chance. She had, in the past, stolen horses from his band often enough to recall hot skirmishes afterward, as she went about her solitary way.

She sighed and turned uphill again, the cradleboard hard against her back. The sun was warm, even at such heights, and she was glad to rest in the shade of a group of aspens, slipping out of the board's harness and setting it against her knee.

Billy Wolf squinched up his small face in the look that told her his diaper was soiled again, and she went through the complicated process of extricating him from his wrappings and changing the smelly moss lining of the soft leather. He was dirty as well as wet, and she used fresh leaves from the aspens and handfuls of dry grass to wipe him clean before powdering him with dust from puffball mushrooms, which she gathered whenever she found them and kept in a pouch just for that purpose.

Once he was clean, she let him lie naked at her feet in the grass, waving his freed hands and staring with interest at the sunlight on the trees, the magpies quarreling in a nearby bush, and Snip, who came frequently to check on his welfare. She sat there for a long time as the sun went down behind the intervening peaks and the shadows lengthened across the countryside.

It was good to rest and think, without the constant need to watch for dangers other than those always present. Her quick ear could hear a snake slithering through the grass many yards away, but he did not come toward her. A hawk called, out of sight and yet audible to one who listened.

Nothing other than chipmunks, busily moving over the stones of the hillside, was nearby; she took the opportunity to raise her shirttail and suckle her son. Billy Wolf nuzzled greedily at her breast, and a vast contentment filled her heart.

She had never thought to have a son—or a mate. A woman warrior was caught between two worlds, neither of which quite fitted her spirit. Those others of her kind that she had heard of, mentioned infrequently but spoken of with respect, had held to the single life, the childless existence, for none of the warriors among her people could quite permit himself to become a "wife."

She was a very fortunate warrior, and she thought with

warmth of Cleve, who was even now trying to be a white man among his own people. But she had an instinct that this was not a natural thing for him. He was not dirty, as those men with whom they had ridden to this camp seemed to be.

Even with the river at hand, the white trappers had not washed, though she and Cleve had gone to the stream in darkness and swum and splashed and scrubbed each other. They had discovered that love was delightful even chin-deep in water, though she felt a bit guilty afterward. If she became pregnant again, her milk would dry before Billy Wolf was ready to eat man-food.

Cleve was not loud and rude, as she had seen others of his people being, as they came through the encampment below. He was, she thought, far superior to any other white man she had met so far.

She heard a step on the hilltop. Someone had perhaps hunted there. She pulled down her shirt, fastened her son back into his cocoon, and turned in the dusk to descend to her own tipi. It was time to cook meat, for even if her man returned too drunk to eat, she was hungry. She ate only once or twice in a day, but feeding the child required that she eat well.

The shadows were inky by the time she came to her camp, where Socks had not been tethered with the other horses, for he was trained to stay nearby and had never run away. She had eaten and was dozing beside her fire when the horse snorted, stamped, and whirled to plunge down the slope toward the turmoil below.

Second Son almost ran after him. Then she realized that she had heard, even through her doze, an echo of Yellow Hair's whistle. He needed the horse to carry something, or he intended to ride out onto the plain. She sighed, cuddled her son to her again under their fur blanket, and drifted off to sleep.

• • •

When Yellow Hair staggered to the tipi, bounced off the door hole twice before he succeeded in getting himself through it, and fell headlong onto the robes beside her, Second Son was quiet, though she had heard his wavering steps all the way up the hill. This was an aspect of her husband that she had not known before, though she had seen others who were intoxicated with the fiery water in those jugs sold below.

It had been hard to make their way through the sprawling camp, because so many early comers had settled in, drunk deeply, and were fighting, yelling, or shooting off their weapons, which was a great waste of their ammunition, to her way of thinking. She could understand that what she saw was most unlike the persons they must have been when normal. Otherwise none of them would have survived for a single moon in this unforgiving country.

She moved over, letting Cleve under the upper robe. His breath was sour with the stuff he had drunk, and she smelled vomit as well. Why should a man so strong and so brave unsettle his wits in this way?

But this was something she could not answer, so she turned her back, pulling the baby away from the lax and heavy body beside her. She closed her eyes and went to sleep again. Tomorrow, she hoped, he would be the person she had known for so many seasons now.

She woke to an agonized moan. Rising onto her elbow, she peered over the great mound of Cleve's shoulder to find his face. It was an interesting shade of greeny gray. His eyes were tightly closed, and he was holding his head hard with both hands as if the top were trying to fly away.

"My God, woman, I never felt so awful in my life," he

groaned. "If that's watered whiskey, deliver me from the straight stuff."

She didn't understand most of that, but she knew he was suffering the same disability she had observed among some of the other drinkers. It didn't seem to be fatal, so she felt he could safely be left to himself. For once, he was dirty, and he stank too badly for her to remain nearby.

Taking the baby with her, Second Son moved outside, where she had kindled her fire the night before. From her gourd she took coals, fed them gently with rotten wood from a fallen tree until they flickered into flame, and started a fresh fire. Something told her that he would want some of the bitter brew his people called coffee, though there was only a pinch left in the poke they had taken from Henri's supplies.

But Socks stood among the alders, nibbling at stray sprouts of grass. He was laden with bundles secured by the thongs that held them to his back. Sudden understanding came to Second Son. This was why his master had called the horse in the evening.

She unfastened the bundles and stacked them before the tipi, rummaging about to find what he had purchased with his furs. The steel arrowheads were a surprise. It hadn't occurred to Second Son that what formed a knife might also shape the tip of an arrow.

Even the best flint arrowheads sometimes shattered on impact. She could see that these deadly things would go deep into a deer, or warrior, or even the tough hide and flesh of a buffalo. She set those aside and burrowed deeper to find the new coffeepot, which charmed her with its shiny surface.

But it was the vast store of food that won her totally. To find such riches waiting here surprised her, for food was something for which warriors and women and children labored hard and long. A winter's store of meat and grass seed, dried berries and nuts and herbs meant day after day of backbreaking work for everyone capable of any sort of labor.

She had never in her life seen a dried apple. The pale, leathery circles felt strange in her hand, but the scent was wonderful, and Second Son decided to taste. Cleve would never bring to camp anything poisonous, she was certain.

She touched the fruit with a tentative tongue, and the sweetness was a shock. There was a mellow flavor behind it as well, better than ripe plums. A nibble confirmed her notion that this was fine eating, and she consumed several slices, though it was not her usual mealtime and her breasts were already heavy with milk again.

A muffled grunt from Billy Wolf brought her back to her task, however, and she soon had the new coffeepot in the edge of the coals, filled with water from the spring she had found farther up the hill. She measured the fresh coffee carefully into her hand, as Cleve had showed her when they first began cooking together.

Before long the little clearing about her home was fragrant with the scent, and in a bit that brought Cleve bumbling out of the tipi, his face still sallow and gaunt, his bright hair soaked with sweat. Without comment (mainly because she had no idea what to say to him), Second Son poured a cup of the brew and dropped into it a cube of sugar from the bag he had bought. Not since Henri's supply ran out had they possessed anything other than occasional wild honey.

He gulped a scalding mouthful, spewed it into the fire, blew carefully on the liquid, and tried again. On his third try he managed to swallow, and as the hot stuff went into him his color returned to something more normal than the deathly pallor he had worn.

He had fallen into her habit of eating only once or twice a day, and she did not expect him to want food. Being sick put one off eating for a time, anyway. But she offered him a circle of the dried fruit so he might clean the nasty taste from his mouth by chewing it.

He grimaced at first, but when he chewed it up and swallowed, a pleased expression crossed his face. "I think I could eat a bit of that. Here, Second Son, you take that new pot and put some water in it. Let it come to a boil and then drop in a handful of apple . . . this stuff. I think that might help my belly to stay put. Right now it wants to roll all over this hill."

This proved to be true. After eating the fragrant mess that resulted, he looked and sounded more like himself. But then, to her horror, he took up Billy Wolf, freed him from his cradleboard, and used the tin spoon to feed him a bit of the stewed fruit, too.

"That is man-food! He is not ready yet for that!" she said, reaching for her son.

"It's all right, really it is," Cleve said. "Ma fed all of us on apple sauce when we was just babies. See, it's soft, and it's sweet, and it goes down smooth. Nothing to choke him on, and it digests real easy. I wouldn't be the man I am without it."

She watched, nervously protective but silent, as Yellow Hair gave the baby as much as he wanted, which was more than she would have believed he would take. Then, his stomach full of warm apple sauce, Billy Wolf drifted off to sleep and his father laid him on his hide rug before the fire. Snip, after sniffing at him and licking a remnant off his chin, lay down beside him, his head on his front paws, his gaze fixed contentedly on his master.

"That's something you won't find among your people," Cleve said, his tone proud. "Of course, I never saw anybody acting such a fool as a lot of us did last night, either. I expect Singing Wolf would put a bug in their ears if they tried making such a shindy as those fellows were doing all night long."

Second Son smiled. "We do not have the fiery water to make us crazy," she said. "I hope that we never do, for our lives are too hard. We cannot waste ourselves so."

Cleve shook his head. "Well, now I've tried it. I didn't like the taste, and I sure as hell don't like the way I feel this morning. Maybe I'll keep the rest of the stuff I bought for trade goods. If we meet some thirsty trapper out in the mountains, 'round about next spring, I'll bet he'd trade a bale of plews for a drink."

She thought of the scattered shapes in the bushes below, snoring raucously, reeking of the stuff they'd been drinking. He was probably right, she decided. Even sick and sorry, Cleve used his head like a wise man. He was no fool like so many of those white eyes who had come here to trade and waste their energies.

She tucked her son back into his cradleboard. "I will go down and look at the things they trade," she said. "How do I manage, if I need something they have?"

He rummaged in his possibles bag and brought out a rumpled tally. "Here. Get what you want. I'll be here, I think. Unless I get to feeling a whole hell of a lot better."

She fastened the board to her back, took up her coupstick, feeling that it would not be necessary to carry her bow here, and headed down the hill. Perhaps this trading meeting was not going to be as uncomfortable for her as she had thought it might be.

The array of goods on display in the sheds was fascinating, although the traders kept a suspicious eye on her. She knew they were having difficulty deciding why a warrior, complete with eagle feathers and coupstick, should be carrying a cradleboard on his back. She had already learned that white men, like her own kind, were suspicious of whatever they didn't understand.

She found a shelf of knives of all sizes and shapes. Fascinated, she bent over the shiny blades, not touching them, but assessing their uses. When at last she reached for one that would be useful for skinning out small game, the trader was there instantly.

"I want this," she said, pointing to the knife. "There is this." She handed him the tally, and he glanced at it suspiciously, looking up at her, looking back down, for some time.

"This's Bear Ax Bennett's tally," he said at last. "What you doin' with it?"

Second Son straightened and fixed him with an iron gaze. "It is also mine, for I am his partner. And his mate. This is our son." She jerked her head toward the baby asleep on her back.

"You're a damn squaw?" he asked, but his voice was shut off as she leaned forward and caught his shirt in one hand, tightening it about his neck until he gobbled like a turkey.

"I am a warrior," she said, her voice almost inaudible. "You will remember that. Now put the marks on this thing so I may take my knife and return to my lodge."

A sudden hush had surrounded them as she spoke, and when she turned with the knife secured in her pouch, she found many eyes gazing at her. Several of the gawkers slipped away as she gazed about calmly and went, without haste, along the path that led toward that up the hillside.

Without speaking, Second Son moved through the crowd, which parted before her. She found that she did not like the way these people smelled or looked or thought. They were dirty and uncouth, without manners or ritual, and she wondered how Cleve had come from such stock without being like these men.

The morning was brilliant, the sun sparkling through chinks in the needled branches above as she climbed again toward her temporary home. There might have been other things down there that she could use, but she was not comfortable among the trappers. When Cleve felt better, she might return with him.

For now she wanted to be rid of the shiny eyes, the lustful glances. That was a thing that only women should have to deal with. A warrior was not patient with such behavior.

There was a thick spinney ahead, and she followed the path around it, not wanting to subject Billy Wolf to slapping branches and the possibility of leaves in his dark eyes. As she rounded the farther side her quick ear caught movement among the slender boles, and she turned, her coupstick ready.

Just in time. A heavy body lurched out of the saplings and grabbed for her. A she struck and sidestepped she felt another presence off to one side, but before she could turn, a pair of huge arms caught her from behind and lifted her from the ground. The stick flew out of her grasp into the bushes.

Second Son had been in tight spots many times before, but this was the first time she had been caught with a baby tied to her back. She had to protect Billy Wolf, even if it meant death for her. So she didn't struggle while those steely arms enclosed her and her son. She went limp, instead.

The arms relaxed, and she pretended to slip down onto the ground. As she went down she rolled, knowing the rigid board would protect the child, and brought up both fists, cracking the man's crotch between them. She felt his testicles give between her knuckles even as he gave a bellow of agony and bent over.

But there were three others, ready and waiting, and before she could roll clear, two of them had her arms and the other was holding her legs. Even so, she managed to get one foot clear and kick a bearded face, spattering blood from his nose over all the rest.

Then they had her down, and she knew a moment of despair. She was not a woman, to be used so. Except for her own man, she had known no other, and the thought sickened her.

Billy Wolf grunted, for much of her weight was now on top of him. As she took a wild bite at a passing hand, Second Son realized that for the first time in all her life she must call for help. The drunken men who had their hands on her had not thought to cover her mouth securely.

Her teeth met in flesh, and the hand was jerked away amid a rain of curses. Then she yelled with all her might, the "Ai-yiiiii-eee!" that she and Yellow Hair had agreed was to be their distress call.

If he was not sleeping too heavily to hear, he would come. And if he did not hear . . . She shuddered, even as she bent her back and tried to ram her head into an approaching chin.

A pair of hands pushed her flat, and one of them, dirty and smelly, covered her lips harshly. Her fine deerhide robe was ripped aside, and hands explored her chest, pulling at the soft leather band she bound about her breasts.

Red rage filled her, blurring her vision, and she struggled insanely, dislodging anyone who tried to position himself above her body. But she knew too well that they were many. She could not struggle so forever, and sooner or later they would have their way. Amid the tumult of the camp her yell had probably not even been noted by anyone.

Then she heard the pound of heavy steps . . . unfamiliar ones. A voice that was more growl than that of many a bear said, "And what're you fellows doing? I think I need to look into this, for you've got the look of sinners in the midst of their sin. You found some Indian wench and are tryin' to have your way with her?"

The pressures about Second Son relaxed for an instant, which was all she needed. She flexed her steel-spring body and was upright, the cradleboard slightly askew behind her but still firmly attached. The baby was grunting, almost whimpering now.

The men who had been kneeling about her were now facing her in an arc, but their eyes were staring beyond her at someone behind. She turned to look and saw a red-faced man whose round blue eyes were sparking with rage.

An unlikely rescuer, she thought, but she did not pause to make his acquaintance. He was a white man, and she didn't trust him, either.

She darted past him and up the slope toward the tipi. Cleve met her halfway, his shirt awry, his hair tumbled, his eyes glazed. "What'samatter?" he mumbled as he caught her in midflight.

"Men. Back there. They tried to do that thing with me. But another came when I cried out, and they loosed me enough to run. Come, Yellow Hair. We must see to the child. He was tumbled about and I lay on him when they threw me down."

He scooped her up and ran with them both back up the hill to their camp, where he laid her tenderly on Billy Wolf's blanket and began unwrapping the infant. For the first time since his first week of life, the child gave a squeak of dismay and protest.

Second Son rolled over and felt him from head to foot, but she could find nothing broken. His face was almost as red as that of the man who had come when she called, but it was more with anger, she decided at last, than with pain.

"Who?" Cleve was running his hands over her, checking for wounds or contusions; he found a number of sore spots but nothing at all serious.

"I do not know these white men," she said. "But I will know those when I meet them again. I have seen their faces, and I will kill them, one by one or all together."

"Not if I get them first," said Yellow Hair. "I'll go down there and see if I can catch up with them right now. You rest for a minute and feed Billy Wolf. He's just about to bust a gut to hold in his crying, I think."

It made sense, and she did as he suggested. The baby was quivering like an aspen leaf in a breeze when she cuddled him to her breast, but the warmth and the flow of milk calmed him quickly, and soon he was suckling contentedly.

She watched her husband stalk down the hillside, his hair bristling with rage, his ears scarlet beneath his pale hair. If he found those men, they would regret it, she knew. But not so much as they would if she found them herself.

She would get them, if they lived, she knew. And they would be entertained in the time-honored manner of her people, with fire and blade and pain carried to its highest pitch.

chapter

— 14 —

His luck had turned after his encounter with the grizzly, Old Joe decided. He lost no more horses and Tarnation was so calm and biddable he almost felt the animal might be sick. But they kept going down out of the mountains, and when the rolling plain stretched before them, he thought they might make it now without more trouble.

He came up the east side of the Sketskedee, keeping clear of the riverside and watching before and behind. He'd come too far to run into an ambush now. In this country you never knew what was around the next bend or behind the next bush.

He could see a distant line of horses beyond the river,

but he was content to wait to reach the rendezvous before making contact with other trappers. Thinking about something like that, he had found, was most times better than getting it.

He camped beside a creek wandering down from the distant heights toward the river, hiding his fire in a gully and his animals among the willows and cottonwoods. He'd get to the fork the next day, he was certain, for he'd traveled this direction before, back when he first came out here to make his fortune.

After a quiet night he was on his way early the next morning, crossing the river at a wide ford. Those others were gone now, probably already there. He figured that this was going to be rowdy and drunken, like the trading forts tended to be when the trappers came down with their plews. Probably some of those early birds were already getting soused.

Joe cleared his throat and spat, and Tarnation flicked her right ear back, then forward, which was her comment on his manners. Damn females—even female horses were too particular. His wife, Mattie, had been a fine woman, but even she had a hissy-fit when he came thumping into their house with dirty boots on or spat into the fireplace. He missed her something terrible, but in some ways being alone was a relief.

As he neared the confluence of the river with the creek, he found to his surprise that there was a large encampment out on the plain. Indians from many tribes he had never before seen together in the same area had erected their tipis and pastured their horses on the fast-dwindling grass.

He spotted several familiar designs—Sun Turns Red was here. Cold Tail's lodge was over at the edge, the thunderclouds dripping rain that was his favorite pattern distinctive on his walls. Arapaho, Lakota, Absaroka,

Pawnee—Pawnee? He wondered what had brought them so far; a dozen other tribes were spread all over the countryside, almost from the river to the mountains.

There was the potential for a large war, Ferris mused, guiding his string clear of the outermost straggle of lodges. Feuds that went back generations were here side by side with people whose favorite pastime was stealing women and horses from each other. If this fellow Ashworth was able to hold all this together without bloodshed, he was a smart man.

When he reached the main camp, he was impressed with its orderly layout. The traders had raised pole shelters for their goods, and behind them was a line of more sturdy buildings. Those had to be to secure the bales of furs, once they were traded.

Ferris grunted with laughter. He could see some sly red-tail like Kills with the Lance figuring out the setup and stealing back his furs every night to trade again in the daytime. These men had foreseen such a possibility and guarded against it.

As he passed the band whose largest tipi held the patterns favored by Sun Turns Red, he glanced toward it and saw the old fellow sitting in its shade. The old Indian lifted a hand in greeting, and Ferris returned the salute. That was some man, he had decided a decade ago, and he'd never had cause to change his mind.

The children who busied themselves around their grandfather's lodge were a new batch, for it had been several years since Ferris visited the Crow band. They stared shyly after him as he turned to glance back.

It made him sad, for he and Mattie had wanted young–'uns and never had one come along. Then, once he lost Mattie, it was as if his rein had broken, and like a loose horse, he headed for the horizon.

Now he was very close to the main shed, his horses

whinnying and snorting behind him, greeting others grazing in small groups in grass patches secured by lines from which dangled bunches of feathers. He felt as glad as they sounded. To see some human faces instead of critters and birds and rocks was a pure damn joy, and that was a fact.

He could smell the harsh tang of liquor as he neared the line of sheds, and before he dismounted, his mouth was watering. He jerked himself up and set his jaw.

Ferris could see one man doing nothing but pouring out jugs of whiskey from a keg in the back of the shed. He could almost feel the burn of the stuff going down his gullet, the puddle of warmth in the pit of his stomach, and he thought with longing of the lightness of heart and head that it brought. But he unloaded his bales and waited patiently while they were checked and tallied.

When the whiskey man came forward with a full jug— "Compliments of Mr. Ashworth, on credit till we settle up"—he took it eagerly.

"I give it up a while back, but that didn't last long," Old Joe said. "Not fittin' for a preacher, I decided. Then I thought, what the hell, a preacher that's got no sins ain't fit to preach."

He led his packhorses and Tarnation away toward a patch of grass. And as he made his solitary camp he kept thinking of the wonderful oblivion waiting for those who drank until they fell and slept. He wouldn't let himself do that.

Being a preacher was a tough job. He often cursed Holy William Kelly for saddling him with the thing, but it hadn't really been the skinny fellow's fault.

A conscience was a miserable thing to have, that was all. Every time Old Joe just about decided to give up and go to hell along with everybody else, he remembered how he felt when he helped cut the little preacher down and sent him off into the wilderness alone. That had been the darkest day of his entire life, and only his decision to take up the calling in William's place had eased his conscience.

There was a small group of men just up the hill from him, bustling about, putting up shelters, spreading bedrolls, cutting wood for a fire. One of those fellows looked familiar.

Ferris rose stiffly, made sure his own fire wasn't likely to spread, and went over to say howdy to them. To his surprise he found that familiar shape to be an unexpected friend, Ernesto Pollino, who was tending the pot over the flames.

"Hey, you little Meskin!" Old Joe shouted, wrapping his arms around the smaller man and lifting him off his feet. "What you doin' here? Last I heard you'd gone back to Coahuila to farm with your papa. He run you off again?"

Ernesto struggled free, smoothed his dark hair and his bright-striped poncho, and grinned up at him. "I go south, *sí*, and I farm with the father and the brother for two year. And then, *madre Mía!* I get so tired of the dirt and the pig and the goat that I think I will blow away like the great wind from the mountain. And I come back and go along with my frien' Tomás, there.

"He have the trap and the supply, and we go ver' far up into the Sangre de Cristos and we catch the many fur. Then come one hombre who tell us about this *tiempo para comprar*. Now we are rich and one day I go back to Coahuila and buy a golden ring for *mi corazón*, Amelita."

"Well, good luck with that!" Ferris sat beside the fire and stared at the younger man, marveling at his luck in finding him again. "You 'member Collis? Big fellow, drank like a whole ocean of fish. He was my pard for a while, but he got caught by the Bloods and they really done him in.

"I . . ." He still had trouble thinking about it, much less saying it. "I had to kill him. He was a goner anyway."

A flash of sympathy moved across the olive-skinned face, and Ernesto nodded understandingly. "The Yaqui, they catch my oldest sister, two years ago. They do bad things to her and at last they throw her onto cactus with her tongue cut out.

"I find her, and when I do, I put my knife into her heart, for she could not live. To see her suffer so—it was not possible! And the papa and mama they never know but that the Yaqui do this thing, as well as the rest."

That was right, Joe thought. "The kindest thing you could do," he said, handing Ernesto another batch of dead branches to lay on the fire. "Now I better mosey along, but we'll get together and catch up on things before long.

"I seen Prevot and Levreaux when I come through the camp down there. They'll have tales to tell, I'm damn sure. But now I just want to move around, see the layout, locate some folks I know, and find out about some I feel likely are dead, now. It's good to be with people again, and that's a fact." He stood, stretched, and reached down to shake the Mexican's sooty hand.

Then he went through the entire encampment, noting numbers in the various groups, hailing those he knew, greeting those he didn't know, and trying to pass a helpful word where he could. With Holy William's fate before his eyes, he knew better than to preach at them, but there had to be a way to guide people right without making them mad in the process.

He went back down to the trading sheds before dark, and he was in the crowd when a short stocky warrior with a papoose on his back came stalking up and bought a knife. When it turned out that this was a woman and the baby was hers, he felt almost dizzy. Women weren't warriors. And warriors didn't have babies. But this one looked both stern and dangerous.

While he puzzled over that the scene played itself out, and by the time he decided it was entirely beyond him, everybody had gone back to business. But the thing still bothered him, and instead of joining Ernesto he wandered up the hill toward the spot where somebody told him this Bare-Ass Bennett she claimed as her partner had set up his camp.

He didn't hurry, and the evening grew darker as he went, so when he heard the yell, he took a minute or two to locate the source. Then he moved as fast as he could up the hill, trying to see any commotion ahead of him.

Whatever was going on, it wasn't easy going, he could tell. Curses and splats of flesh on flesh came to his ears as he approached, and once he got close enough to see a bit, even though the aspen grove was now pretty dark, he could tell that several men had taken down that high-headed Indian woman who called herself a warrior. Three were holding her down while the fourth tried to get on top of her, which he didn't seem to have much luck doing.

He didn't hold with women of any kind, these days. One who thought she was a man shook his mind to its depths. But this was rape, and the Book was strict about fornication. These men were endangering their immortal souls, and it was his job to save them from themselves. If he saved the woman, too, so be it.

When she dashed past him and out of sight, he was glad. He didn't want to have to deal with her at all, though he knew there was further work for him in that situation. This Bennett was putting his own soul in jeopardy, too, and that would have to be seen to.

Freed of that immediate problem, he leaned against a tree and looked down at the drunken and disorderly crew left in the clearing of smashed saplings and disturbed leaves. "Boys," he said, "I can see you've got some things to do some thinking about, and I'm the man can help you understand them.

"I don't hold with women, though I can be partial to a drink, and I don't blame you a bit for bein' set on fire by a female. They're the source of all sin and trouble, but you're supposed to be strong enough to resist 'em. And I'm going to tell you how, so you sit right down and listen hard, because if you don't, I'll knock your heads together."

Four sets of dazed eyes glanced about at the other tattered would-be rapists and back at Old Joe. One of the men leaned back against a sapling, slipped sideways, and began to snore, but the rest sank into the leaves and looked receptive.

That was just as well because he had taken off his worn deerhide shirt and flexed his muscles, ready to carry out his threat. When he finished his sermon, some hour and a half later when the spinney was too dark for him to see his congregation, he didn't know if they'd taken it in or not. The snorer was out of it, of course, but the other three had looked dazed and sick in about equal parts. Now they were silent.

At last Old Joe sighed mightily and straightened. His back was cricked from leaning against the tree, and he felt sure those fellows' butts were sore from sitting on roots and broken branches. Maybe he'd done some good and maybe not, but at least he'd tried. Maybe Bill Kelly would approve, wherever he was.

It was too late when he left the spinney to tackle this Bennett who was cohabitating with a squaw. That was high on his list of things to do, but he figured a good night's sleep wouldn't come amiss. Joe had known squaw men before, mostly Frenchies, and he knew what a task lay before him. There must be something about redskin women that hooked a man deep.

Or maybe, he thought as he rekindled a blaze beside his bedroll, it was just having somebody to do the camp work, skin out game and beaver, and keep your back warm at night. Whatever it was, men seemed to need women around, even in clean new country that ought to be clear of such complications.

He set his coffeepot in the edge of the coals at last and covered over the glowing pile. In the morning there would still be enough heat so his coffee would boil quickly and dry branches would kindle at once. But he had to do it all himself . . . he snorted at his own foolishness, took a long pull at his jug, and rolled up in his bearskin. The nip never left the air at these altitudes, summer or winter.

Thunder woke him. He opened one bleary eye and scanned the patches of sky above the treetops over his camp. It was gray and heavy looking, fat with rain at lower elevations and snow at higher ones. Thank God he was down here, out of the high country that could get snow in August, if things fell out wrong.

He heaved himself up and set the flap to keep the rain off his bed and his fire. By the time the thing was stretched tightly between four fairly well-spaced young trees, it was beginning to billow in the rising wind that brought a smell of rain on summer grass.

Below, in the distance, he could hear whinnies as the horses pastured on the plain grew excited by the coming storm. His own string, which he had moved into a small glade above his campsite, was beginning to wheel and shake their manes. He would tether them to trees if they got much more jittery.

Once he secured his shelter, he built up the fire again, waving away the smoke that curled under the hide roof before finding its way out from under. By the time he had his horses tied, his pot was boiling, filling the air with the fragrance of fresh coffee.

With the hot liquid in him he felt more human. He gulped several tin cups of the steaming brew and chewed some jerky for his breakfast. He knew he'd need strength for the task that lay before him.

The wind whistled through the needles of the pines and whipped the alders until green leaves flew. Ferris hunkered under his roof flap, nursing his fire as the cold rain pelted down and thunder boomed overhead fit to shake the ground beneath him.

From time to time lightning jagged down to meet the heights to the south, and once a bolt seemed to take aim at the flatland below, flashing and booming almost simultaneously. A frantic squeal from Tarnation made him thankful he'd secured the animals, for she had a habit of running away in storms and coming back only when it suited her. The last time she'd come back pregnant, he found months later, and he wondered darkly what infernal stallion she had found in the depths of the range.

When the thunder had walked away over the mountains to the south, the rain set in in earnest. It looked as if it were there to stay for a while, so Ferris donned his deerhide robe and his wide, flat hat and set out up the mountain. It was pretty certain his prey would be in their camp, with this going on.

He walked a long way. They'd moved very far up the hill, and even the nearest of their neighbors wouldn't stink up their air with shit and smoke. He had to approve, though he did it grudgingly. He would have done the same if he hadn't been so lonesome for company after his months alone.

The tipi was the Cheyenne style, its walls down and secured, the flaps set to carry smoke away without letting in the rain. As it wasn't cold, the door hole wasn't laced shut.

A curl of smoke from the smokehole told him Bennett and his woman and child were settled in for as long as it rained. That was good . . . he'd get the whole business done with and go about finding someone else who needed straightening out.

"Yo!" he yelled as he came into the skimpy cleared space around the lodge. "Anybody home?" The greeting reminded him painfully of the infrequent visitors who had come to see him and Mattie on their remote farm. But he shook away the memory and kept his mind focused on his duty.

A blond head was thrust through the door hole. "We're home. Come in."

"That's not cautious of you, boy," Ferris said as he ducked through and sat beside the small fire centering the shelter. "There's men here would cut out your liver and fry it over your own fire, if you given 'em a chance."

Bennett thrust out a hand. "Cleve Bennett," he said. "You've got to be the preacher that saved my wife. We know there are hard cases here, but Ashworth has them pretty well under control, I think. Emile says anybody makes trouble will get run out and can't ever come to any rendezvous again.

"What happened to my wife last night was bad, but they were drunk. Things like that happen, and I heard what you said to those drunks. I went down to kill 'em all, but you already were busy, and I listened to what you said. Made me think about what my ma taught me, back in Missouri."

A great satisfaction filled Old Joe Ferris. If this boy had a Christian mother, then there was hope for getting him loose from his red-tail woman.

Cleve poured soup in a gourd and handed it to him. "Here, you probably need something, with all this chilly rain. Second Son gets rabbits and woodchucks and grouse, and we put together a soup that will curl your hair." He sipped his own gourdful and sighed with satisfaction.

"You know, if you hadn't had those men hog-tied with your talking last night, I'd have killed the whole crew. I was mad enough to bust, you'd better believe. And when I got through, if there were any left, then Second Son would have had their scalps on her belt. She was even madder than I was."

Ferris relished the rich stew to the last drop. But when he set aside the gourd, he noted that the woman, instead of moving about quietly serving the men as Indian women did, sat still and listened, her expression stern. Except for her occasional concerned glance at the baby, who was rolling on a hide rug with a dog, she showed no visible evidence of being female at all.

He wiped his mouth on his sleeve politely and belched. "Mighty good stew," he said. "And I'll not say it wasn't welcome. But I come up here to do a job. It may hurt your feelin's, but it's got to be done. You got to quit livin' in sin, son."

Much to Ferris's surprise Bennett burst into laughter. "You preachers! Every one's the same, no matter who he is or where he is. Man, we're married. We've been married for a long time."

Ferris shook his head. "The mumbo jumbo the Injuns do, that's not legal and moral. It may satisfy the poor ignorant wench, but it don't hold for a white man. This has got to end and you got to put her away."

The woman ignored him as if wasn't there at all, but

she turned her intense gaze toward Bennett. "This is what he meant, then?" she asked.

Cleve nodded. "Yep, this is just exactly what Holy William had in mind when he insisted we get hitched legal. He knew white men and he knew what it'd take to smooth things over. You get the paper, will you, Second Son?"

She moved, but Joe was staring at the young man in stunned astonishment. "Holy William? That wouldn't be Bill Kelly, would it? Where is he? Is he all right?"

"You knew him?" Bennett asked.

"Knowed him, hell! He's the reason I'm stuck with bein' a preacher and having to squash down all my human nature!"

"Well, he *was* all right for a while there, after we rescued him from the Indians. He'd had a rough time of it, though. After he was run out of his trapping camp, he was a captive and a slave for a while. But after we got him loose, he seemed real happy for as long as he lasted."

"Then he's dead." Joe felt a sudden emptiness. In some pocket of his soul he had hoped the skinny fellow might still be alive to give him his forgiveness. Without that, life wasn't going to get any easier.

"He got killed in early spring. We were trapping a deep valley that we thought never had been found by anybody, when Jules Terrebonne's great big sidekick got the drop on me. If it hadn't been for Holy William, we'd all have been goners. Second Son there was on the point of having Billy Wolf, and it took us both to stay alive.

"But Holy William died right there, shot by Terrebonne. We left that Frenchman tied to a tree in the snow and went back home. We buried William at his feet, and his bones make his grave marker."

The woman handed Ferris a bit of paper, much creased and rather greasy. He unfolded it with fingers that threat-

ened to shake and found himself looking down at marriage lines. The signature was quavery, but he recognized
Bill Kelly's scrawl.

By damn, this time there wasn't anything to solve. This
couple, red and white, were joined in the holy bonds of
matrimony, and he didn't have to worry about saving
either one of them!

The woman smiled at last, and the warmth of that
smile went right through him. Maybe this was one woman
he could get along with.

chapter

— 15 —

When an ambush failed, it was an embarrassment to the leader who planned it. Though Many Badgers and Shot His Own Foot never mentioned that abortive wait beside the river canyon for victims who never came, Kills with the Lance felt the disgrace as a stab in his heart.

He had gathered his kin and those of the band who wished to see the white men's rendezvous on the morning after his return to the camp, and they had traveled swiftly toward their destination. A captive Ute woman, wife of Shot His Own Foot, knew this country well. She led them unerringly over high passes and down wooded slopes to a point from which they could look over a plain and see many tipis, many horses, all spread at random over the summer grass.

Beyond, where the hills rose to meet the heights to the south, there was motion, too. As his group drew nearer, the keen eyes of the warrior made out pole huts, squared instead of rounded, and even more people, most of them alien in look and walk.

Some wore wide hats of leather, as some of the Fransay did. Others, he saw as he came near, used animal skins to cover their heads, as his own people sometimes did in winter. Fox jaws gaped above tousled hair of unnatural shades—red and yellow and the brown of winter leaves.

Gazing about at the other camps, he saw that the Hunkpapa were there, along with many others, most of whom were or had been enemies of the Pawnee at one time or another. It was best to set up his own camp far from those most likely to make trouble, for here Kills with the Lance found himself among too many strangers to risk violence.

He sent his small daughter, Smooth Dove, to listen at the nearest of the tipis, where several children ran about amid a rabble of dogs. Though men felt themselves to be the ones who knew things, he had found that the women and the children often knew more things more quickly than anyone.

He had used his child before to learn what he needed to know, and now he waited patiently while his wives raised the tipi and his father fletched arrows with stiff fingers beside him. When Dove returned, she was smiling, her face sticky with honey that she had been given when the other children received chunks of comb.

"This is a good place," she said, settling into her father's lap and wiping her hands on his knee. "Those women gave me sweet, and their son and daughters told me about this big camp."

"And you must tell me," said Lance, surreptitiously wiping away the honey with a handful of grass. "What did they say to you?"

"They told me that a great white man called Ash has come with many wonderful things to trade for fur. Weapons of metal, like the knife you carry, and food like nothing they ever tasted. Firewater that makes the men happy and causes them to sing and go to sleep."

"But how does he keep all these tribes from fighting or raiding for horses?" Lance asked her, his gaze fixed on the distant blur that was the pole sheds where he had learned the traders' furs were stored.

"He says that anyone who starts to fight must go, and he and his family will never be let to come back to any trading again, wherever it is done. Already the white men have sent away Pointed Teeth and his band, because they raided Sun Turns Red's camp and stole horses."

Lance had to admit to himself that this was a smart way to keep the peace, though it meant that he must bide his time. If he found those he hunted, he could do nothing against them here. But if he did find them, he thought, smiling and smoothing his daughter's hair, who was to control what he might do later, when the trappers left the rendezvous?

But first he must learn if they were here. And among so many whites, who were all bearded and dirty and smelled like mountain sheep, how was he to recognize two whom he had never seen from nearby? That was his next problem. What he might do about them could wait until later.

"There are fine things there in the sheds," Many Badgers said to him. He had come softly from behind the tipi, and Lance turned toward him, wondering that he had already managed to see the white men's store.

"We have skins," he said in a cautious tone. "Wolverine, wolf, fox, buffalo, lynx, and beaver, but they were for our own winter warmth. Do the whites take other skins than those of the flat-tails?"

"They are trading for all kinds of furs. They look at them very closely, and they only want those that are smooth and thick-furred. We have fine pelts, my brother. Our women dress skins as well as any and better than most. We do not have great bales of them, as the white trappers do, but we might have enough to trade for many useful things."

Kills with the Lance felt a warmth grow inside him. While he was here to do something else entirely, it would be good to return to the tribe with shining metal tools and weapons. Bird on a High Branch, who was the leading chief of the Pawnee now, would open his skeptical eyes in admiration if they returned with supplies of things that could not be made by their own people or traded for with other tribes.

"We will go and see what they have," he said, rising to his feet. "Perhaps even the children will find something they need, if we have enough furs."

As they moved toward the sheds he felt strangely uncertain. This was a situation that he had never faced before, and though his courage had never been questioned, he felt his heart give a flutter as he swept his gaze over the busy crowd of men and the strange array of things laid out on the boards.

A very old Blood came to meet them, holding up his hand in greeting. The babble of alien talk around them told Lance that it was going to be hard to make himself understood if these whites did not understand sign, but the ancient warrior spoke to him in his own tongue.

"Welcome, Kills with the Lance, to the trading place of the great Ash. I am called Snow Weasel, and I speak the tongue of the white men. I know of you from tales told by your enemies. The white men have sent me to speak with all the tribes who come, for I have learned many languages in my long life.'' His tone was pompous and a bit arrogant, but Lance kept his face still.

"It is good to have words as well as sign, when one has important matters to discuss. We understand that this man Ash takes hides other than those of the flat-tail. We have a few that we might trade, if he is willing and his things are useful.'' He watched Snow Weasel's seamed face without seeming to, but reading that creased map was not an easy task.

"Come with me to speak with Broken Hand, whose white name is Mackay. He trades for the white man, and his word rules here.'' The old man turned majestically and moved toward the largest of the roofs set on poles, where a short, square man clad in a strange pink garment, stained and grubby, above his waist, and leather leggings below was arguing with one of the other whites, their scarlet faces almost meeting over a roll of rare white fox furs.

"Ye scroungy scut, I'd be a great fool to risk so much on a set of mangy fox hides! Beaver is what we came to get, and that is what we will give top price for. For these''—he gestured down at the silken hides contemptuously—''you get what I offered and not a hair more.''

Strangely, the other did not seem discouraged. "You will give what I ask, or I shall take these fur to the Hudson's Bay Company, who will offer the price that is just.'' The voice was French. The face, half-concealed by a voluminous beard and straggles of graying hair, was familiar.

This was the one called Prevot, who had ranged the plains and the mountains for half Lance's lifetime. The man had visited Buffalo Grass more than once and was welcome in the lodges of the tribe. He was not one to be cheated in a trade, and the Pawnee stood silent, waiting his turn and watching intently as the dickering went on. The words were not understandable, but the gestures and the tones were, and he learned much.

The Blood murmured into his ear, "This one is of Ash's own men. He has no fear of being cheated, but I think the white men simply like to shout and haggle."

That was Lance's impression as well. When his turn came, he turned to Snow Weasel and spoke slowly so the old one could translate easily.

"We have come far to trade with the great Ash." That wasn't entirely true, but politeness never came amiss. "We have in our camp many hides and furs of all kinds, wolf and lynx, fox and beaver, and buffalo and cougar.

"If you will trade for such furs, we will bring them to show you. If you will not, we will ride away in peace." That sounded very dignified and self-confident, he thought.

The old man spoke briefly, and the red-faced one looked thoughtful for a long moment. Then he nodded and replied, his words sharp and brief.

"Broken Hand says that he will look at the furs the Pawnee bring. But he does not promise to buy them." Weasel's eyes crinkled at the corners, their normal creases deepening very slightly.

Ah. That attitude was the sign of a shrewd trader who made no promises. Kills with the Lance nodded and turned, as if indifferent to the Blood's translated words.

He gazed up the slopes of the surrounding hills, which were spotted with tent flaps and the conical tops of tipis. He looked back down across the grassland, which swarmed with people and horses. If nothing else, this was going to be interesting, and it might prove profitable as well.

Many Badgers spoke quietly at his shoulder. "We have

not seen those two we pursued in the high country. How will we find if they are here?"

Lance inclined his head, his stiff roach of hair that ran up the middle of his shaven skull catching the breeze blowing in from the lowland. "We will listen. We will learn the tongues of these men, but we will not let them know that.

"Go back and ask Snow Weasel to visit our camp tonight. We will share meat, in gratitude for his service, and we will ask him questions."

Badgers almost smiled, for he had been Lance's friend since they were boys snaring rabbits and practicing their marksmanship on small birds on the plains. He understood better than anyone, Lance knew, the workings of his mind.

A day spent wandering among the many camps and people gathered at the fork had waned at last. Kills with the Lance returned to his tipi, where Leaps Like a Rabbit had food ready in her pot and a fat woodchuck dripping spits of grease into the fire.

The wind, once the sun went down, was cool, and the walls of the tipi were laced down to hold in the heat, as the family gathered around the blaze, their faces ruddy in the warm light. When Snow Weasel arrived, he seemed pleased to be seated beside Buffalo Grass in the place of honor while the women served him bowls of stew and chunks of hot meat.

By the time they had eaten, the mood of the group at the fire had grown mellow and cheerful. "It is not often that we entertain one of your people in this manner," Buffalo Grass said at last. "But my son is glad that you spoke for him to the trader. If you would like to choose a fur in payment, we will be pleased to make a gift to you."

Snow Weasel grinned, his cheeks wrinkling danger-
ously and his toothless gums pink in the firelight. "Many
of my people have died beside your fires, and many of
yours at ours. Yet this is a new time. These white men
make changes in the old ways, as others have done
before them. Because of that I will take your gift.

"My fathers tell of a time when other tribes roamed
the prairie and hunted in the mountains, but now
they are gone and your people and the Tsistsistas and
the Dakota take their places. Our people have lived in
the wide country since the gods made the grass, and we
pushed you back when you came, time after time. At last
we could no longer resist you, and now here you are."
He chuckled, though Lance could not understand what
he found so amusing.

"These white-eyed ones will not be different. They
come now with trade goods and gifts and the firewater
that turns men's minds. They will come, in time, to take
this land from us. It is in my mind that if all our tribes,
even those that have warred for many lives of men,
would band together and slaughter every one of them, it
would be a good thing."

Buffalo Grass stared into the fire, and Lance knew it
was a courtesy so their guest would not see the skepticism
in his eyes. He felt the same. This was wild talk; was Snow
Weasel one mind-touched by the gods?

But the old man sighed. "I know this will not happen.
Perhaps it is only the dream of an old man who has seen
too much blood, too many deaths, too many raids and
scalps hung on lances, but I would know peace before I
die."

"If you dislike the whites, why do you talk for them
with those who come to trade?" asked Kills with the
Lance.

"I do not dislike them," he said. "Some are not bad

men, though all are childlike and foolish at times. No, they are brave, and they learn quickly the ways to live in our country. It is that, I think, that troubles my heart.

"They learn too quickly. And they know things that we have never seen or thought about. Their thunder sticks, for instance, are a marvel, even though one can shoot many arrows while a white is putting the food into his weapon and pushing it down with a stick.

"I have seen the one they call Levreaux kill a moose with one shot, from a distance so great that you would doubt the accuracy of my eyes if I spoke of it. Those weapons have a far longer range than any bow, I promise you. A warrior with arrows or lances would be swept away like dry grass before a devil wind, if he faced many men armed with such things.

"No, I can see a time when we will be pushed aside by the white men as if we were grass on the plain. It pains me to think of it." He accepted the pipe that Weaves Baskets had prepared, puffed on it, and started it on its circle about the fire.

Long after he had left the fireside, Lance thought of his words. The old were wise, everyone knew, but from time to time one grew dreamy and foolish. He hoped that this was one of those, for he had no desire to make war on men who commanded the thunder.

Only one white man and his companion deserved the attention of the Pawnee here at the fork of the Sketskedee, and that one had to be here. It was only a matter of time until Kills with the Lance discovered him.

Many Badgers had not been mistaken when he said the furs they carried were well treated and beautiful. The rolls piled on several of the horses the next morning were limp and silky, and when Broken Hand opened them, the pelts glistened in the sun, every hair clean and glossy.

After reading the inscrutable faces of his own kind all his life, Kills with the Lance found this white's features easy to decipher. Mackay's eyes widened when he drew out the shining beaver furs, which had been brought back from a winter hunt by Lance's own hands. The others were as fine, for the women of his band were skilled at such work. And the pelts themselves had been prime, taken at the height of their condition.

The process of weighing the furs puzzled him as it was done, but Snow Weasel explained that they would be paid according to the weight of the goods, rather than bartering piece by piece. When the weighing was done, it was time to bargain, and Lance always enjoyed that. The white man's lips thinned, and Lance knew he was about to offer some trade that was unworthy of consideration. When Snow Weasel spoke, the Pawnee shook his head.

"This is not a price; it is a child's game. But I do not feel playful today, so I will take my poor furs and return to my camp. It is plain that we cannot deal with the great Ash and his men." Without waiting for his words to be told to the trader, he turned and stalked away while the women, who had come with him, approached to reroll the furs.

"Now wait a minute!" He did not know the words, but Lance understood the tone precisely. "Don't be too hasty!"

Weasel's translation was unnecessary, but Lance waited, his head cocked attentively, until the old man was done. Then he deliberately looked thoughtful for a very long moment before turning back to the shed.

The dickering became intense, the trader's offers being translated hastily by Weasel. Lance countered each with a reasonable decline in his demands, until at last they met in a suitable compromise.

Then the women took the tally, which Weasel explained to them with great care, and moved among the sheds, using the credit thriftily to buy things they could never make for themselves. Iron pots and spoons were a marvel to them, and even a warrior could see the great usefulness of such for cooking. From a distance Lance kept a watchful eye on them until he was sure they were not wasting anything.

As he turned, satisfied at last, toward the place where the firewater was being dispensed, he saw, moving away up the hill, a tall, broad shape topped by bright hair. Was this the one he had hunted for so long? Surely it was! The dog at the man's heels looked just like the one that had fled with those who had escaped him in the mountains.

He moved with well-concealed haste back to the shed, where Weasel rested in the shade, his eyes closed. "My friend, do you know that man?" Lance asked, gesturing toward the now-distant trapper, whose yellow hair gleamed, even so far away, in the sunlight.

Weasel squinted and peered intently. Then he nodded. "It is the one with the Tsistsistas warrior/wife. I have seen them about the camp, but they have their own tipi high above, where it is quiet and their spring is not polluted with the shit of horses and men. They call him Ben-nat. It is said that he once killed a bear with one of those metal woodchoppers they have."

"This wife—you say she is a Tsistsistas warrior? I think I have known of her, back in the wide country. There are few women who raid and hunt. What is she called?" A conviction was growing within Lance that here he had found not only this new enemy but a very old adversary who had stolen horses from his people and never been punished for her audacity.

Revenge for many old raids was in his hands. But he must go carefully, for he did not intend to be cast out of this great camp until he chose to go. He must study those two from a distance, set children's eyes to watch their tipi, think hard about his long-awaited vengeance.

There was time for all of that, because he had been told that this rendezvous would last for weeks. When his plan was made, then it would be time to have the women pack everything on their travois.

They would follow him away as if satisfied with the time spent here. Only his enemies would know, at the last, that Kills with the Lance had taken his revenge.

chapter

— 16 —

Once he recovered from the combination of his hangover and his initial anger, Cleve found himself intensely interested in the gathering Ashworth had managed to bring together. His first need was to find his wife's molesters, and he set his mind to that as much as he could. But though Second Son examined faces closely, she had not yet recognized those who had attacked her.

Joe Ferris, too, was keeping a lookout, but he had no luck, either.

As he hadn't seen the culprits, Cleve had no hope of locating them for himself, but he kept hoping as he moved about the rendezvous, greeting old acquaintances from the Ashworth enterprise and finding new friends.

The newest of these, of course, was Ferris himself, and Cleve found himself reminded often of Holy William as he got better acquainted with the self-styled preacher.

Emile Prevot and his band welcomed him, too, and often Cleve made his way down the hill in the evening to chew the fat awhile over their fire. When that happened, Second Son frequently took Billy Wolf and went down into the plain to visit the various bands camped there. The chance to meet, on this truce ground, with so many of the plains and mountain people intrigued her.

As Cleve strolled down the hillside in the flickering darkness punctuated by the gleams of many distant fires, he thought that she would, in time, make a fine peace chief, like her brother, Singing Wolf. He stopped in his tracks, stunned by his own thoughts.

He was taking it for granted that they would remain out here among the Indians. Though he had intended, when he first lit out from Missouri, to come home again someday many years in the future when his father might be safely dead, he found that this was no longer a thing he wanted. The thought of going back to the hard labor of the farm, the grim religion, and the habits of his own kind made him cringe.

Even here among white men, he sometimes felt uncomfortable, though these trappers were far more like the man he had become than anyone he could think of back home. Even Prevot and Levreaux, who had seemed so mature and sensible on the trip up the Missouri, showed themselves to be randy old drunkards when it came down to the money.

He had met them staggering up to their camp, roaring with laughter or bawling French songs that sounded obscene even to one who didn't understand the language.

He knew they had visited the tipis on the plain, where

there were tribes whose women were not so virtuous as the Tsistsistas. Some families considered the gains to be made by selling the services of wives or daughters to be well worth the trouble.

Second Son was not shocked; she had known all her life that different tribes held to different ways. But Cleve had been shaped by his Missouri upbringing, the psalm-singing religious fervor that laid down strict rules for human behavior, and thought anyone who didn't observe them to be lost to hell. That troubled him, for in that area he felt his wife to be more mature than he was.

He had not been tempted to visit any of those distant tipis himself. Even though Second Son held him at arm's length now, in order to keep milk flowing until their son reached an age to eat what she called man-food, he hadn't strayed. After his warrior woman, those pliant, doe-eyed creatures below were too tame for his taste.

Besides which, he thought, stepping into the firelight and greeting Prevot and Bill Shooner, if he did go down there, he'd probably best keep right on going. He didn't want to think what Second Son might do if he took one of those other women. He had heard grim tales of the ways in which Cheyenne women dealt with captured enemies, and he suspected that they had gotten off light compared with what she would do to him.

But it was pleasant sitting drinking coffee with those who were resting up from the excesses of the days and nights before. Prevot looked exhausted but smug, and Bill seemed less haggard and drawn than he had before.

"Been a great time," Shooner said. He slung the dregs from his coffee cup into the fire, amid a great crackling of sparks, and filled it again from their new pot, which was already growing dull from the soot of the open fire.

"I've seen folks I never thought I'd meet. It's been

good. Better than good. But I—I guess I've been alone too long. It's almost time to head back into the high country. Somehow, the drinkin' and the hellin' around don't seem so fine, once you're in the middle of it."

Emile snorted. "You have the mountain fever, true and sure," he told the young man. "You have lose much there—the brother, the sense that you will never die, which the young they always carry with them. But you have find something else, I think.

"It come to me ver' long ago, when I first come here from the south. I go into those mountain, smell the air so clean and sharp it cut the lung, and I feel big like the mountain. Like the sky, even. There I am the king more than ever *le pauvre* Louis was, before the Revolution remove him."

Cleve nodded. That was the way he was beginning to feel, as if only in the high lonely was he truly a free man. With Second Son and Billy Wolf, he was not alone, which made it even better. He found it in him to pity Bill, for losing a brother must be a terrible thing.

That brought his own brothers to mind. How were they faring, back there in Missouri, still under their father's iron hand and will? He felt guilty suddenly, as if he had no right to run free and leave them to suffer the thing he had escaped.

Emile interrupted his musing, and he lifted his head, trying to catch the drift of the Frenchman's words. He had mentioned a name. . . .

"Did you say Kills with the Lance?" he asked. "Sorry, I was daydreaming and didn't quite catch what you said."

Prevot coughed hugely and spat into the fire. "*Oui*, the Pawnee leader. I see him below, near the trade shed. He have bring fur to trade, I think, though it seem to me that he have not prepare for such a thing as this. The fur, they are fine, but they are not enough to pay him to come so far.

"I wonder what that wily one have in his mind? Mischief, I would wager, *mes amis*. He is capable of much of that, for I know him of old, when he was ver' young in the tipi of his father, Buffalo Grass. He have disappoint his father greatly, I think, because he will not think ahead."

Cleve narrowed his eyes, thinking hard. If the Pawnee had come to the rendezvous without being prepared for serious trading, it was likely that fur was not what had brought him here.

Many among the mountains, he had learned since his arrival, had spread the word of the gathering, so it would not have been hard for the warrior to find out about it. What would be more likely than that two trappers with laden horses would be heading here?

"We ran into him, back along a ways," he said. He accepted a refill and shifted his tin cup between his hands until the heat waned a bit. "He came up behind us as we crossed a pass; we got away, but not without leaving some of his men dead behind us. If it hadn't been for Second Son, I don't know if we'd have escaped at all."

Prevot shot a sharp glance in his direction. There was a worry crease between his grizzled eyebrows. "That one, he is the ver' bad enemy. He will follow one who trouble him until he find him, as I see with these eyes, back in the plain. You have kill some of his men? He is surely here looking for you, *n'est-ce pas?*"

"I figure it that way. But Ashworth has a pretty tight rein on what goes on here. Maybe that will keep the peace."

"Do not rely on that, Cleve. This Lance, he is smart and he is patient. Keep the watch while you are here, *sans aucun doute,* but also when you leave be more cautious than ever in your life. He will find the way, but it will be subtle and it will be clever.'' Emile leaned forward in his earnestness, his hands moving emphatically, cutting the air with decisive gestures.

"I have think, just now, that your warrior woman have had the dealing with that Pawnee in the past. I have hear the tale among the tribes concerning her raid for the horse. She have steal the Pawnee pony many time, and it is from the band of Buffalo Grass and his son that some were taken. So it is not only with you he have the quarrel, but with her.''

He leaned back, worry now clear on his face. "I have play with your son, Cleve. The *bébé*, he is smart and he is strong, for one so young. You mus' keep him safe. Warn the wife, I ask you strongly. Keep the watch, for if that warrior cannot attack you, he will do what he can to harm one you love.''

Making his way up the hill later, Cleve found those words ringing in his head. He had no doubt that the Frenchman was right and Kills with the Lance was here at the rendezvous. That being so, he felt that he and Second Son should leave soon, very quietly and without fanfare. Those who had attacked his wife had surely left the rendezvous, he felt, to escape their wrath. That left them free to give up the search.

They could do as they had before, disappearing into the trackless reaches of the mountains before Lance could know they were gone. Getting the horses together would be no problem, for he had never grazed them down in the grassy pastures beside the stream. Smaller glades among the firs and pines near their tipi were sufficient to keep their animals under their eyes.

He checked on them before moving to his and Second Son's quarters and rebuilding the fire before the door hole. It was too quiet, here alone, after having his family about him. Again he shivered, thinking of Bill Shooner trekking away into the mountains alone. It was a chilling thought.

He sat in the glimmer of the fire, waiting for Second Son to return from her trek into the grasslands. Snip had, as usual, gone with her, which was a comfort. That dog was as much a partner as any person he knew, just about, and he trusted him like his own right arm. With this new information he was particularly glad to have those alert ears and that sharp nose with his wife and son.

A step sounded on the path below, and he stood and reached for Second Son's bow, which hung inside the tipi. "Who's there?" he called.

"We come," his wife said, stepping into the light. "Is Snip with you? He ran after a rabbit, and I have not seen him since. That is not like him."

Cleve felt a chill run down his backbone. Emile had warned him, but he had not dreamed anything might happen so soon. While Ashworth would take any move against his family very seriously, the theft of a dog would be something the Pawnee could manage to get away with without much risk of being sent away permanently.

"Did you know that Kills with the Lance is here?" he asked his wife. He took Billy Wolf from the cradleboard and set him on his blanket before the small fire. The child stared about as if looking for his playmate.

Second Son dropped to her knees beside Cleve. "He did not come to you?" Her voice was tense. "I saw one of the Pawnee's wives below, so I knew they were here. But why would he take the dog? He has many dogs of his own!"

Cleve stood and began to arm himself. "Emile told me, just a little while ago, that this particular Pawnee would do anything he could to take revenge for those men we killed back there at the pass. He can't risk any conflict with you or me, and he sure as hell can't threaten the baby. Any man here would skin him alive for that.

"But what's to keep him from taking Snip? If he's been watching us, he knows how much we think of him. Most of these trappers and traders don't know he's anything but just a dog, though, and I figure Lance is smart enough to know that.

"If I go down and make a big fuss about losing him, get into a fight, maybe, or kill somebody, I'll be the one making trouble and neither of us will ever be allowed at a rendezvous again. We can't afford that, but I hope I'm at least as tricky as Lance."

Second Son's dark eyes glimmered almost red in the light from the fire. She had on her "war" face, grim and determined, but he shook his head.

"You got to stay here with the baby in case we're mistaken and Snip comes back. Besides, I can get away with stuff you can't, with this bunch, and we've got to be cautious. I'm going down and sneak up on that damn Pawnee. If Snip's there and alive, I'll bring him back."

"He is becoming old," said Second Son. "I have seen that he lags behind when we travel, rather than running all about us looking for scent. He"—she looked suddenly sad— "may not be alive now. Be prepared for that."

Cleve had seen the same things as they crossed this last batch of mountains and plains. The bounce was gone from his dog's step, the alert gleam from his eyes, though they seemed to miss nothing, even now.

"Even if he's dead, I'm going to bring him back. No damn Pawnee is going to eat him if I can help it." He felt a lump rise in his throat and he swallowed it down with sheer willpower.

"You take care. If you feel the need, go down and sit with Prevot and his bunch till I get back. I don't know how long it'll be. You keep a close watch, you hear?"

She nodded, and he turned into the shadows. Above him an owl quavered a long cry into the night, and far off up the hill another answered. He listened closely, for he felt there might be a chance that the Pawnee had set a watch on his tipi, but those were not the voices of men, however skilled at imitation.

The camps were settling for the night, the groans of drunks already getting sick from their excesses mingling with raucous snores and mutters from those already asleep. Even this clean and isolated place had begun to stink of men.

Fires had been damped, and the night was very black. Only his frequent trips up and down the path to his camp allowed him to slip, unheard, past the others who had chosen this hill for their campsites.

When he came to the creek below, he paused and listened hard. To his right were the sheds, where guards patrolled constantly. A fortune in fur was stored there now, and the trade goods, depleted as they were, commanded even better prices than before. Latecomers to the rendezvous were going to pay through the nose for necessities, Cleve knew.

He heard the careful steps of a guard, a murmured comment as two met at the ends of their patrols. Then he turned toward the creek, looked both ways to make sure that no one would see him silhouetted against the pewter gleam of the water, and stepped down from hummock to hummock, descending the bank to the stream.

Halfway down he froze. Something large and clumsy thrashed through the willows, alders, and reeds below the spot where he stood. When he heard it begin to retch, Cleve smiled and waited until the drunken man stumbled away and out of hearing.

Again he crept downward, and this time he reached the water without incident. This was a spot where men came after water, for the slope was gentle, and the stream was swift enough so the water was fairly clean.

Cleve had waded out to check its quality before they found the spring above their camping spot, so he knew the creek was shallow here. He could wade across without trouble, for the snow water had diminished with the depletion of the snows on the mountains.

The burble of the stream across the stones in its bed hid any soft splash he made as he went in to his knees, his waist, his chest. Then the uneven bed leveled out somewhat, and he managed to cross without more than a couple of slips that threatened to dump him entirely into the icy water.

The other bank was thickly grown with bushes and small trees, for those camped beyond it were at some distance and took their water from the river. That was just as well, he thought, as he wriggled up the slope and peered out from the shelter of a chokecherry bush.

Some thousand yards from his position he could see the conical shapes of tipis. Two years ago he could never have distinguished the Sioux style from the Pawnee or the Cheyenne, but now he saw immediately that these were Arapaho.

He had to go around them, for Emile had told him that the Pawnee raised their tipis farther to the west, at the edge of the Indian encampment. But already dogs were stirring, raising questioning yips and growls. If they took after him in full cry, he would never be able to creep up on his goal.

He slid back down and crawled along the bank, just below the top, for a long way. As the creek went somewhat westward, he knew that eventually he would be able to bypass the danger of the dogs. But this was difficult, and the chance of making noise was great, for the bushes and small trees had dropped generations of dead wood, which tended to crackle and snap loudly beneath the weight of a man.

He had to test every spot on which he must rest hand or knee, working aside any brittle twigs before putting his weight down. The stars, now visible above the open country, moved inexorably westward, and he began to wonder if he would cover the necessary distance before dawn put an end to the possibility of finishing his task.

But he could not hurry, and he did his best to keep moving even after his hands became raw and sore. Sharp rocks, thorns, and prickles added their own peculiar torture to his progress, but at last he crawled up and saw, some quarter mile distant, the shapes of the Pawnee lodges.

There would be dogs there, too, but he just had to chance them. Cleve lay flat and wriggled forward, taking care to make as little sound as possible. From time to time he flattened to the ground as some restless animal growled and scratched and settled again to sleep.

Far away toward the mountains in the south there was the lonely howl of a wolf, and Cleve thought longingly of his brother Singing Wolf. With a few of the Tsistsistas to help him, he could snatch his dog back and be gone before anybody was the wiser.

At last he came near the central tipi, which he thought must be Lance's, as it was a bit larger than the other three. Emile said the man had two wives, several children, and his father living in his home. That would take some space.

The dogs, to his relief, were sleeping near the warm ashes of the fire that had been built in the center of the rough circle formed by the tipis. That allowed him to get right up behind that larger lodge without being betrayed by a chorus of barks.

He slipped his new knife, a marvel of keen-edged steel, from its sling and slit the buffalo-hide covering of the shelter slowly, taking care not to let the blade sing against the tough leather.

Though the fire did not burn high enough to glow brightly through the tipi's walls, there was still a glimmer among the coals in the center of the space inside. So dark was the night that it was not long before Cleve's eyes adjusted and he could see the sleepers lying about the curving interior of the shelter.

Flickers caught reflections from polished quill beadwork decorating breastplates and robes hung on the walls. Shields and bows caught the light in glimpses. After a time he could see that there were two long shapes . . . men, obviously. Two smaller ones must be the wives, and four others differing in smallness must be the children Emile had told him about.

Where was Snip? Or was this even the right tipi? Or had they already killed him and eaten him for supper? Grief filled him at the thought, and he almost rose and tore into the lodge like a wounded grizzly, to search for his dog.

But he didn't intend to make a fuss big enough to ban him from the trading meets in the future. No, he had to do this with all the finesse he had learned from his wife and her kindred.

He had to out-Pawnee the Pawnee, which according to Second Son would not be that difficult, as she had done it all the time when she was younger. She had given away dozens of horses stolen from this very man and his band.

Cleve moved silently around and cut another slit, gaining a different angle on the interior. This time he could see an indeterminate bundle lying beyond a pile of baskets and pots at one side of the tipi. No one slept near it, for the floor was cluttered with tools and equipment.

It might be Snip, but it was perilously far around toward the place where the band's dogs whimpered and quivered in their sleep. He paused for a long time, trying to find an alternative, but at last Cleve moved toward that side of the shelter so slowly he felt the short journey would never come to an end.

When he slit the hide wall that time, there was a thin shriek of friction, and one of the sleepers half rose on an elbow, listening. It was a long time before he settled back into his blankets, and even longer before his breathing told Cleve that he was again fast asleep.

When the slit was wide enough, Cleve reached through, his long arms a blessing, and touched the bundle. It was so wrapped about with thongs and bark netting that it was a moment before he realized that it was warm and furry beneath its bindings. Snip! It had to be!

He drew it toward him, careful not to upset any of the pots nearby, working the dog through the slit and out into the starlight. Once he had him safely free of the tipi, he took his knife and cut a lock of yellow hair from his head and put it on the floor where Snip had lain, setting a pot to hold it. Lance would know who had taken the stolen dog, though there was nothing he could do about it.

There came a muffled whine from the bundle he had rescued; it was the merest thread of sound, but it caught the alert ear of one of the camp dogs. Cleve went flat to the ground, covering Snip with his body.

The dog rose stiffly and sniffed about the tipi of its owner, evidently, for it was not the one beside which the two fugitives cowered. It gave a halfhearted growl and turned around three times before settling down again.

Breathing again, Cleve backed around the curve of Lance's lodge and began the long crawl back to the shelter of the creekbank. By the time he rolled over into the concealment of the bushes again, the eastern sky was pale with dawn, and the dogs in the Pawnee camp were up and about.

He had made it by a hairsbreadth, but that was enough. He paused now to untie his dog, and Snip shook himself, sneezed irritably, and staggered about for a moment until his legs would work properly again.

They couldn't see each other clearly, but Cleve caught the old dog into his arms and hugged him tightly. Snip's tongue, newly wet from a long drink in the creek, licked his cheek with moist affection. Then the two of them crossed the creek, deeper here, so they had to swim a bit, and started the long trek back to Second Son and Billy Wolf.

Behind them, out on the grassy land, there was a clamor of barking. Voices grunted in Pawnee.

Cleve grinned. Kills with the Lance must have discovered his prisoner missing. He would have found the taunting sign left by the rescuer. The Pawnee would be seething with rage, but there was nothing he could do. Not here; not now.

Later? There was no safety in these wild lands. Tomorrow would be another problem, to be solved when it came.

chapter

— 17 —

It was a good plan, Lance thought. He had watched his prey cautiously, making sure that even the Tsistsistas warrior did not discover his observation. His small daughter, Dove, was his best spy, able to wander about the camp of hairy-faced whites without anyone noticing her at all. She had done this for days before she learned what he wanted to know.

Dove brought him the news that this warrior with the yellow-haired one was his old enemy of the Cheyenne. There was a baby, she said, and he longed to steal it and raise it as a true Pawnee, brother to his own small son, though the laws of this place forbade that.

Buffalo Grass had taken pains to make sure he understood this, for he was much taken with the notion of trapping furs and trading them for the many fine tools and luxuries the white men had brought. "Our lives will be easier if we can use the metal knives, the bright arrowheads, and the warm blankets of bright colors. Do not risk our future for vengeance, my son."

Those had been his words, and Lance revered his father. His life had been shaped by his desire to please the older man. Lance would take care, but he would have revenge, nevertheless.

Dove had told him about the marvelous dog that obeyed words from the two she watched. "It cares for the baby," she said, "and keeps him from crawling into the fire. It seems like a person, not like a mangy dog, full of fleas and noise."

Lance had thought for a long time about that as the trading proceeded and trappers arrived with fresh bales while others departed with empty packhorses and heavy heads. He had not arrived at his position easily, for he had a habit of risking too much before giving it much thought. But now he had a plan.

The child could not be touched—not yet. But who was to say that a dog was of any worth other than as meat for the pot or a warning in the night? He had never known anyone who cared for an individual dog, and among the white men he saw no dogs at all, except for this single one. He would take that animal from those who valued it.

It would, if nothing else, be an inconvenience to them. And if they were wise, they would know that this was only the first move in a long and complicated dance.

Second Son understood, he was certain, and she would explain it to this white man she had married. No matter how small this first step, it could do nothing but disturb those he intended to destroy.

He sent his two nephews, when the time was right, to capture the animal, for small boys ran through the camps of all, red and white, like grasshoppers. Naked and dusty, they could not be identified as to tribe, and nobody paid the least attention to them.

The boys returned sometime after dark with the struggling dog bouncing between them. They had stolen thongs to bind him, but he was snapping and growling furiously, nevertheless.

"Put him inside the tipi," Lance said.

The two did as they were told and accepted his quiet word of praise without comment. They liked to steal things, and a dog was as good as anything else, he knew.

Once he looked at his captive, Lance wondered that anyone could possibly find him different from any other of his kind. He was old, his eyes beginning to dull, his ears uneven, his coat rough and full of burrs.

Those eyes lit up fiercely when he bent to turn the dog over. Lance barely jerked his hand away in time to avoid a lunge to bite that almost dislocated the animal's spine.

It wasn't safe to leave any part of him that could move, so the Pawnee bade his younger wife to net him firmly. Then he sat before his fire with his father, who was himself bright-eyed with pride, for once in his life.

"This is a good thing," the old man said. "They will not be able to drive us out, even if they know who has taken him. And there are big cats in the mountains, wolves on the plain. Things happen to dogs all the time, and no one notices."

"Yes," said Lance, his gaze fixed on the coals, his mind ranging forward to a time when one or the other of his enemies might roast in a fire hotter still. "And if they come and protest, we will go to the greatest of the white men and make complaint, as some of the others do. That would be a fine joke."

But he did not smile. That was not his way.

He awoke with first light, feeling something amiss. The dogs outside were snuffling and panting and whimpering as if something had disturbed them, and he rose and bent through the door hole. Nothing could be seen except the first line of dawn marked across the heights to the east.

Only when he returned to his tipi did he think to check on the dog. The animal was gone as if he had never been. But where he had lain, a pot had been placed. Lance kicked it aside in a clatter of utensils and stared down. There was something on the ground where the pot had sat.

He bent and felt about, finding a wisp of fur—or hair? He took it up and moved to the firepit, feeding the coals to a blaze. Then he stared down at the lock of hair between his fingers.

Yellow hair gleamed in the uncertain light. That warrior had reclaimed his animal before he should have known it was missing.

Lance rose to his full height and yelled shrilly, venting his anger in a series of yips to the new morning. Buffalo Grass came upright with the speed of one much younger.

Both of the wives sprang up and seized their knives. The children crept to the walls of the tipi and kept silent, their eyes wide and frightened.

But Lance was too lost in his fury to notice. This was an insult worse than any the Cheyenne woman had visited upon him. Everyone stole horses and women; that game was old and familiar. For one to steal from beneath his very nose, out of the lodge in which he slept—that was unbearable. To leave such a token to prove who accomplished this coup was so bold as to still the breath in Lance's chest.

Blood must pay for this insult. Even if he could steal the dog again, that was no longer acceptable. Body to body, weapon to weapon, he must attack those who had killed his men and insulted his home.

But before that happened, he must make them suffer worse pain of body and spirit than anyone had ever known. All the long history of Pawnee torture, back to the time before his people abandoned sacrifice to the gods, would live again when he had those two within his grasp.

And before that time there was always the child to consider. He knew as well as anyone how even a warrior suffered when his young sickened or were in danger. Those people would learn all the long chants of grief for a lost child before they came to their ends at last.

And that child—he almost smiled with the elegance of his plan—would grow up to be their bitter enemy.

chapter

— 19 —

The itch was back. Joe Ferris always thought that this would be the last time he'd head back into the mountains, taking with him his guilty conscience and his load of worry about the souls of those he'd met when he came down among his own kind, but it never happened.

With or without a companion, he found himself compelled to stare northward more and more often, something inside him pulling him toward those distant, uncaring peaks. When that happened, he rounded up his packhorses, saddled Tarnation, and said his good-byes as briefly as possible.

This time it took a bit more doing, for he had taken a real liking to Cleve Bennett's baby. It had been years since he'd been with young'uns, and this dark-eyed little so-and-so had reached out and grabbed him by the heart. That was going to be a wrench, he thought as he climbed the hill for a last visit before taking off into the blue.

Second Son was sitting beside the fire, her fingers busy fletching arrows. Billy Wolf was rolling on his blanket with Snip, their limbs so entangled that it was hard to tell where one began and the other left off. Ferris looked around for Cleve, but he wasn't in sight.

"Greeting, Joe," the woman said. She made a gesture of welcome and pushed the coffeepot nearer the coals. "Yellow Hair has gone down to settle with the traders. He wants gold, instead of trade goods, for the part of the tally we have not used."

"Good thinkin'," he said. He dropped onto a pine stump and stretched his feet to the blaze. Midsummer or not, he was beginning to find that the high country chilled his bones right down to the marrow, and any fire was a good one.

"I wish I'd've had the sense to do that back when I was young and feisty and had a future ahead of me instead of a past behind. I could've saved enough to ride in a carriage and carry a gold-headed walking stick."

Second Son looked quizzical, and he realized that she hadn't any idea what he meant. "One day you two may want to settle down. Maybe with your folks, maybe not. But whatever you do, there's going to be white men comin' thicker than flies, and sooner than later. You're going to need cash money to deal with 'em, because that's the onliest thing they understand or respect."

Her eyes lit with understanding. "That is so. I have seen it here, with these who are not, I think, much like those they left behind beyond the great river. But they do nothing useful with the coins they get. The things are pretty, but you cannot eat them or shelter under them when the snow flies."

He laughed. She was a one, all right. Cleve had done a good day's work when he hooked up with her, for she had a head on her shoulders, and she'd keep the boy straight, one way or another. Ferris had noticed that Bennett had never gone by night down to the Indian encampments, and he chalked up one for his wife for keeping him out of that den of iniquity.

Heavy steps climbed the path, and Ferris rose to greet Cleve. "Here, boy, let me help you with that," he said, taking one of the heavy bags Bennett carried. "Land o' Goshen! What you got in here, anyway?"

Cleve grinned and looked about to make sure there was nobody within hearing range. "I bought me some horseshoes," he said. "They're heavy, but I noticed the unshod critters having trouble with split hooves and such."

He sat down beside the preacher and leaned close to his ear. "And if there's some gold down in there among the iron, why who's to know? It's all heavy, and it clanks just about the same."

Ferris felt a gust of laughter shake him. This was one smart young fellow, there was no denying that.

"Well, you be careful anyway, you hear? There's men can smell gold if it's ninety feet deep inside a hill or under a river. And most of 'em'll kill or die tryin' to get at it, too."

He sighed and accepted the tin cup Second Son handed him. The hot liquid was strong and bitter, and he thought regretfully of the months he'd spend using roasted acorns after his own supply ran out. But it was time, and there was no gainsaying it.

"I come to say good-bye," he said. "It's time for this child to take off again. I got a hankering to see the

Tetons again. That's just about the last untouched country up there, and I sure as hell couldn't have worse luck than I did the last couple of years, now, could I?''

Cleve nodded, his face sober. "We're thinking about leaving ourselves. Since I took Snip back from the Pawnee, I've been feeling eyes on us all the time. I meant to go right off, but then I thought it won't make much difference.

"If he's got somebody watching us, they'll know, no matter what. But you're right. It's time. I'm getting sick of man-stink and whiskey and tall tales that are going around for the tenth time."

"Right! So I'm off. If you two wander up that direction, you might give a whoop and see if I pop up out of the bushes. I'd be mighty proud to see you and the young'un again."

Joe emptied his cup and sighed mightily. Then he rose and bent to scoop the baby up in his thick arms. Billy Wolf gurgled with laughter.

Ferris handed the child to his mother, touched Snip with a gentle toe, and turned back down the hill. "You take good care of 'em," he called back to Cleve. "Or I'll have somethin' to say to you when we meet again."

His heart was a bit heavy, but he knew that dragging things out wouldn't help anything. He found Tarnation snorting with impatience, knowing that she was about to take off into the wild country again, and when he mounted her, he felt a surge of excitement. He never knew what he'd find out there in the lonely stretches of grass and the jagged peaks.

The Tetons . . . what Second Son called the Ghost Mountains. They were like that, pale, keeping their heads mostly in the clouds, rising like visions ahead as you rode down from the ridges to the east.

He kicked the mare into motion, and the pack string

tugged on the rope as he headed along the path toward the ford.

"Whooo-eee!" yelled Ed Fellmore as he passed. "You old catawampus, don't you know you ought to be settin' in a rocking chair instead of trappin'?"

"I'll wipe your eye next time, Ed," Joe cried. "By God, I'll bring back the finest batch of plews ever saw in all the world. If I'm older than you, it ain't by much, and anyway it only means I know what I'm doin'. These mossy-eared younkers ain't a patch on me when it comes to trappin' a beaver stream."

A chorus of insult and boasts followed him until he crossed the ford and came to the trail, now packed hard as any road in the east, that led north. He wouldn't follow it far before turning west again, heading for Bear River.

He passed through the camps, nodding a solemn greeting to old men sitting in the shadows of their tipis and to young warriors who were obviously plotting mischief to come, once the strict law of this rendezvous was behind them. But at one time or another he had met most of them, and he had helped those he could.

Old Joe Ferris had little to fear from the Indians, whatever the breed, for they all considered him more than a little mad. That gave him an idea, and he turned abruptly toward the heights to the west so as to pass within easy distance of the lodge where Buffalo Grass lived with his son.

The old leader was standing beside a horse, examining a cut on the beast's hock. Flies buzzed about them as Ferris pulled to a halt.

"Looks like he got caught in the brush or a sticker-bush," he said, dismounting and bending to look. "I got some salve in my pack that might help him out. You want I should try it?"

Buffalo Grass stepped back. "I greet you, Feh-ris. Your medicine has helped us in the past. I will be glad if it cures this animal, which is my son's favorite."

Ferris grinned inside where it didn't show as he wiped the greasy stuff onto the wound. It would keep off the flies, and the pine rosin in it was a healing thing, he'd found over the years.

"There, that ought to do it. He's a good animal, I can see. Lots of spirit, like that son of yours."

"You will sit and smoke a pipe with me?" the old man asked, bending to enter the tipi.

"Sure will." Ferris joined him, sitting cross-legged before the empty firepit. It was too hot, down here on the plain, for even old folks to need a blaze. "But I'll be goin' pretty soon. Just stopped by to say good-bye. I'm headed out again, back to the beaver and the high places."

"Soon we will go, too, I think, when Lance has completed his task. We will go east to our homes."

The dark eyes looked a bit sad, and Ferris wondered if that meant that Lance might go someplace else. Was the sneaky bastard going to try to ambush Bennett again as the young fellow took his family back into the mountains?

He decided to take his time. There was a lot to see between here and the Ghost Mountains, and trapping wouldn't begin until late fall anyway. If anything happened and he heard about it, he'd like to be in a position to do some good for his friends.

Buffalo Grass qualified as one of those, but Lance had always been a young piss-ant, and he hadn't changed a bit once he was grown up. No, Ferris would be on watch along his backtrail, for he'd had a notion that Cleve intended to come behind him.

He grunted his thanks as he finished his last puff on

the pipe, handed it to the old man, and rose. "I'll see you when the time is right," he said.

Buffalo Grass looked even sadder, as if his ancient heart had read things he couldn't possibly know. "If I live, and if you return. Good hunting to you, Feh-ris."

It was only when he was well on his way, the clamor of dogs and horses and children left behind, that Ferris wondered if there was a hidden warning in those words. He shrugged and kicked Tarnation in the ribs. Warning or not, he'd do what he thought was right, and be damned to anybody.

chapter

— 19 —

When Ferris disappeared down the path, the alders whipping back into place behind him, Cleve felt a sudden emptiness. Though he hadn't realized it, he had in some way depended on Old Joe to keep a weather eye on the other trappers, as well as on the Pawnee.

Not since Holy William died had he felt such confidence in another man. Emile and Paul and the other Ashworth trappers were good men, in their ways, but they were focused on their own projects and problems. They were handy in a fight and fun to be around, and that was good. Yet since the birth of Billy Wolf, Cleve felt a need for more eyes to watch, more ears to listen.

For the first time he had a sound understanding of the

need for a tribe around him, for mutual support and protection. The Indians had the right idea. Every man was his own boss, but every family pulled together without protest when things got tough. The chiefs were not rulers but wise men who knew how to plan for the future and to provide for their own. An incompetent leader was quietly ignored and another put into his place.

It was time now for his own tiny tribe to leave this confusion and chaos. Old Joe had mentioned going into the Ghost Mountains, and Cleve remembered his brief glimpse of those snowy heights as he crossed a high pass in the Absarokas. That would be a good place to go.

The summer still stretched before them, and their own valley waited, already familiar, for the winter's trapping. They had no need, as yet, to scout out new beaver streams. There was time to explore. Even Second Son had gone no nearer those wraithlike peaks than he, and she seemed anxious to see new places. Once they arrived, a friend would be near at hand.

"I am a coward," Cleve said to Second Son as they bound supplies, new traps, and pots and tools and weapons onto the packhorses. "Since the baby was born, I feel a threat always hanging over us. I never was afraid of much of anything before, but now . . . It's bad to be scared."

She stared up at him, her dark eyes thoughtful. "I never knew what it was like to be responsible for a small one," she said. "It never occurred to me how hard it is for a woman, armed with unfit weapons, burdened with perhaps a baby on her back and toddlers holding on to her leggings, to deal with danger. Those lives are so fragile, little sparks so easily put out."

He shivered, for that was his own feeling when he held his son or watched him play with Snip. So much of his heart was bound up in that tiny package of flesh and bone, and perhaps that was the thing that frightened him.

"No, you are no coward, Yellow Hair," she continued. "You are a father. I suspect that all fathers feel the same, and all mothers. We cannot let our fears control us, and so we deny them and keep our faces calm. Yet now I know that those old ones I thought had no feelings simply knew how to keep them buried in their hearts."

It was dusk, and the camp below, its groups of late-comers feeling the end of this rendezvous approaching, was a turmoil of shouting, gunshots, and drunken laughter. Cleve no longer felt any excitement, one way or the other. He had come and he had seen. Now it was time to go, once the night fell thickly enough to cover their departure.

He had asked Paul Levreaux to scout his camp from a distance and to signal if anyone watched. There had been no signal, so he felt that any spy was either too clever to be noted or Lance had sent no one today.

When at last he led Socks along a path that skirted the side of the hill toward the west, avoiding the usual route down to the water, he never even noticed the tiny girl-child crouching under a bush.

Once they were clear of the last camp, the air smelled cleaner. It was now dry, for July had almost gone and the heat and lack of rain had turned the grasses tan. The creek was shallow when they forded it well upstream, and Cleve knew water might be scarce until they reached the mountains again.

They filled their waterskins at a spring that trickled from beneath a rock before leaving the stream. Then they set out across the grasslands toward the uneven spine of mountains rising to the west.

Cleve did not hurry. Second Son showed no impatience, either, as they moved across the vast open spaces, the dried grasses brushing their horses' bellies as they trampled through the deep growths. Few buffalo came into these interior prairies, and elk and moose and deer did not flatten vast areas as the herds of big beasts did. Now and then they found a wallow, only a few house-sized holes worn into the soil where the big beasts cleaned their hides with grit, but nowhere was there one of the mile-wide complexes of wallows like those found on the plains.

From far away on a western breeze there came a fragrance of something tangy, and Cleve sniffed appreciatively. Second Son laughed, her voice sounding younger, freer than it had in weeks. A great weight seemed to have been lifted from both their hearts, and they grinned at each other and kicked their mounts into a gallop.

The dry wind fluttered Cleve's hair about his ears, and he felt the surge of Socks's muscles with joy. They were alone again, free of the noise and stink of the rendez-vous, free of the constant company of those who, however well liked, were not always welcome. The mountains ahead called, and Cleve felt a sudden urge to race toward those jagged peaks and hide among them like a fox going into his burrow. Perhaps there his child would be safe.

The pounding of Shadow's hooves behind him told him that his wife felt the same wild impulse. Behind came the thunder of the packhorses, lightly laden, who seemed intoxicated with this new freedom. Snorts and whinnies came from the string, and some kicked up their heels or danced sideways on the lead rope as they followed. Only Snip, running beside Socks, seemed hard put to keep up.

Soon Cleve sobered and slowed the pace, and they stopped to rest the animals, but still he felt the pull of the

heights, and they moved by night for a long time, until
the moon set. That night Second Son opened her arms
to him, compelled by this new privacy, and when Cleve
slept at last, drained by her warmth and strength, he did
not dream.

They moved up through shallow hills that grew steeper
as they approached the mountains beyond. Once among
those, they turned north, with heights on either hand,
though the route here was not steep. A creek, fringed
with tall trees and willows, alders and pines, afforded
them a good route into the country they sought.

As they went they found great faces of rose-colored
stone rising to the east above the creek. On the left were
rounded slopes, but to the right the heights seemed
sliced from top to bottom by the knives of giants, their
bared faces glowing in the warmth of sunset light.

Cleve wondered if the cathedrals his mother had told
her sons about when he was small might not have looked
like that, tall and shapely and awe inspiring. Second Son
stared upward, silent and wide-eyed, and Cleve felt the
same sense of wonder.

The creek wound intricately, its snakelike route shadowy and the soil beneath damp. Fish flirted in the shallows, and Second Son managed to net several with the
netting she had traded for with the Crow at the rendezvous. They ate the crisp flesh on the sticks with which
they had spitted them over the fire, and even Billy Wolf
licked a bit of the meat, trying to suck the flavor and
making chewing motions.

"This is a good place," Second Son said, leaning back
against a rock and gazing into the flames. "There are
beaver. There is water. Many plants grow here, and those
I do not know I could learn to use. But this is not a place

that I could love for long. I need the plains, Yellow Hair. Will you go back with me, one day, to see my people?"

Cleve nodded. "I intended to, all along. Billy Wolf needs to know his kinfolks. His grandpa would like to see him, and Singing Wolf would just about go crazy, though he wouldn't show a sign of it. We'll go back, maybe next summer. No need for a rendezvous every year, unless we're more than lucky with our traps.

"I want to see everybody again anyway. Your nephew Cub must be about grown by now. Going on raids and all sorts of devilment. I'd like to see that youngster again. I owe him a lot for teaching me to use a bow like a Cheyenne instead of a clumsy white eye."

The next day they moved upstream again, struggling through thick growths of cottonwoods, alders, birches, and chokecherry bushes. It was tough going, but they kept on long after nightfall. In such a tight cleft it was impossible to go wrong, and only when they and the horses were pretty well exhausted did they pause.

On the third day they came over a steep ridge and looked down on a lake, huge, blue as a sapphire, beautiful as a dream. Amid the arid tan of the surrounding hills the water beckoned to them all, and Cleve dismounted to lead the horses down the steep slope.

As they neared the water he saw something move beyond a growth of trees and bushes, and he halted and dropped, knowing that Second Son had probably already taken cover. The horses huddled together around Socks, and Cleve crawled forward to take shelter behind a ridge of rocks.

Below, the scene was peaceful, quiet, inviting. Then a square shape stepped out of its shelter and looked up toward them.

"Youuuuu, Cleve! Come on down. I got camp all set

up and stew on the fire. 'Bout time you showed up! I been waitin' for three days now.''

It was Old Joe Ferris, big as life, his chunky form familiar and welcome. When you expect an enemy and find a friend, Cleve had learned the hard way, it's the best sort of surprise.

"You old buzzard! You got me going for a little while there," Cleve called back.

They led the horses down carefully, for a broken leg meant they must kill the disabled animal, and that meant being short a packhorse when next they brought their bales to trade. By the time they had the string dipping their noses into the water, the smell of stew and coffee was teasing their noses.

Short as the time had been since Ferris left the camp, Cleve found himself more than happy to see the old fellow. They sat about the fire that night, while Billy Wolf pulled himself up by Old Joe's knees and tried to walk across the blanket to his mother. If the child had been his own grandson, the preacher couldn't have seemed more pleased.

Snip, who slept more and more nowadays, woke and kept a sharp eye on his baby. Finally he lay between the child and the fire, though it was obviously hotter there than he found comfortable.

"That old dog, he's about the best I ever seen," Joe said, reaching to pat Snip's head. A thump of the skinny tail implied appreciation, but the dog didn't respond as he usually did to affection.

"Seems as if this last trip has worn him down a lot," Cleve said. He frowned, remembering the frisky animal that had followed him away from his home in Missouri, four years ago. This was a very old dog, and he could no longer hide that from himself.

"Might ought to put him on one of the packhorses,

when you take off again, and let him ride as far as he'll hold still for it." Joe spat into the fire, and a sizzle and sparks rose from the coals.

"That is good," said Second Son. "The dog is a friend, and he watches the baby. We must keep him well for as long as we can."

They spent three days fishing in the blue lake, swimming and splashing in its shallows, wandering along the slopes and finding new plants that even Second Son could not identify. This was the free time of the year, when no compelling task pushed them forward.

Cleve almost forgot his unease, for with three sets of eyes to watch, plus Snip's unerring nose and ears, they felt safe from enemies. Yet the time came when they had to move on toward the Tetons, following the river feeding the lake until it hooked off toward the west.

"There's a long valley that'll take us right to the Snake," Ferris said, when they camped the first night after setting out. He drew in the edge of the ashes with a twig, marking parallel lines.

"Them's the mountains; not big 'uns, just nice reg'lar ones that's not too hard to cross, if you get caught in a pinch. There's creeks and woods and all kinds of game. Fat country, full of food and fuel. If I was a settlin' man, I'd stop right there and spend the rest of my life livin' off the land."

"Will you do that, when you get too old to go up and down mountains and trap in freezing weather?" Cleve asked him. That prospect seemed inviting, even to him.

"Won't be able to." Ferris sighed and stretched his legs to the fire. "You watch, boy. In ten years' time there'll be folks poppin' up all over this country, plowin' the ground, cuttin' the trees, messin' up everything just the way they done back east.

"Why you reckon I come out here in the first place? Once my wife died, I was free to leave, and I never took no stock in the things folks done anyway. Farmin' is for fools. Towns is worse. Who'd want to set in a store all day, writing little squiggly marks in a book?

"Long as these old legs will keep going up one hill and down another, I'll keep on the move. When I stop, it'll be all to once, and for good, I reckon. I want to lie down under a pine or a fir tree, on the clean needles that've been fallin' since God was a baby, and shut my eyes and draw a last breath that don't stink of shit and somebody else's cookin'."

He was serious, his face drawn into wrinkles of earnestness, his eyes looking into the distance as if they saw his own death just as he described it. Cleve felt a pang of loss and almost laughed at his own foolishness.

"You're not that old," he said. "Besides, if a grizzly doesn't get you, a Blackfoot may. Like your partner, Collis. It doesn't look as if many folks die of old age out here."

Ferris laughed. "You got that dead right," he said. "Now let's turn in, because we've got a long way to go before we get to them Ghost Mountains. They're . . . they're like nothin' I ever seen. Not like any mountains you ever thought on. The Frenchies call 'em Tetons, but I like Ghosts better, though they're more like great big angels, standin' there on the edge of the world, staring out through the clouds and thinkin' about things we can't even imagine. That's where I'll turn off. I'm goin' around t'other way, over into the country west of the Rockies. Got to see some new country, before I get too old."

The distant glimpse he had caught of those strange mountains on his way down to the fork had not suggested anything like angels to Cleve, and as he took up the first watch he thought about the man's words. He'd had a funny feeling, that was true. It had subsided when they stayed beside the lake, but now that they had left behind its blue expanse and were again bounded by mountains, that feeling returned.

He ranged upslope, keeping a wary eye on the camp below. Though the fire had been damped and only blots of shadow showed where the blanketed figures slept, he had an unerring sense of its location. He made a wide circle, coming down to cross the creek they were following and climbing again beyond it.

The moon had waned while they dawdled at the lake, and only the stars now kept him company. Far in the north he heard a rumble of thunder, and as he kept watch a bank of cloud crept in from the west. Tomorrow would be wet.

The stars wheeled westward, and when the constellation he called the Blacksmith touched the rim of dark peaks, he went down and woke Second Son to take his place. She was instantly awake, as always, and before he could speak, she sniffed the air, stared up at the sky overhead, which was already streaked with long fingers of cloud, and nodded.

"Rain. Before dawn. I will help you raise a tent flap, for there is no need to sleep in the damp." She was as good as her word, and before she crept away, Old Joe, Billy Wolf, and Cleve had shelter.

The pounding of rain woke Cleve after hours of sleep. Ferris was gone about his rounds, and Second Son was snuggled, naked, against him. She must have gotten soaked, for the drum of water on the tough hide overhead spoke of a deluge that had continued for some time. He turned and drew her into his arms, laying his cheek against the smooth crown of her head. She smelled of damp hair, wood smoke, and clean air. Drifting into sleep again, he was conscious of a vast thankfulness and an even greater worry that troubled him even while he slept.

chapter

— 20 —

The Pawnee rode north and east, with Buffalo Grass on his steel-gray horse leading the band. Lance watched his family move away over the tall tan grass, his heart following the small shape of his daughter, who trudged along amid a tangle of dogs.

His body remained stubbornly rooted to the trail of his enemies. This was, his father had often told him, his worst fault. He could not look past his immediate concerns to see the long path of the future and the best interests of his people.

"You will never be a war chief or a great leader, my son, for you will not put aside your own desires. You cannot look past the little things that trouble you to see on the horizon the dust of the great troubles you must avoid.

"Go, if you must, after those warriors who killed our people. But remember that you would have killed them. It is not wrong for a warrior to defend himself."

"But one was Second Son of the Tsistsistas!" he had objected, feeling his face grow hot with angry blood.

"Indeed. I have talked long with others who camped at the white man's trading, and they have all lost horses to someone, over the years. We steal horses from the Tsistsistas. Why should we protest when they do the same to us? It gives the young men practice at war, and it is great sport. Seldom does a raid for horses lead to bitter war.

"You cannot say that even in her last and greatest raid this woman/man killed anyone. She counted coup upon the fourteen-summer youth who guarded the horses, and then she took the herd. A great feat, even in an enemy, and I honor her for it. She left the boy unharmed and accomplished her purpose. You also should honor such deeds."

Buffalo Grass seldom spoke at such length, and never did he rebuke his son before others. This was his father's last chance, Lance knew, to caution him in private before he left the family and set off alone into the reaches of those alien mountains on the horizon.

Why did he hate the yellow-haired man so much? He had not even known that the warrior's companion was Second Son until later, so her raids on Pawnee horses had not influenced him.

Perhaps it was the cleverness of the trap the white man had laid. Kills with the Lance had fallen into it as if he were a youth just provided with man-arrows and a full-length bow. His clumsiness had allowed those two to escape his raid on their bale-laden pack animals.

Now, riding west and north, he thought of the wonderful things his people could have bought with the furs that Yellow Hair had brought to the rendezvous. Few trappers had arrived with more or better furs, and the thought of such plunder escaping from his hands made Lance grind his teeth and push his horse even harder.

Once he had determined the direction his quarry took, he did not follow their trail. It was plain that they were wandering, seeing new territory, in no hurry to reach the northern streams where beaver was prime. From the general course they took he knew that they must come, at last, to the valley of the Ghost Mountains.

He had listened to the talk in the camp, learning white-man words so that he could understand without betraying the fact. They had come from the north, probably from the Shadow Mountains. It was likely they would return there, once they finished their wandering through new country. And if they stopped to make a new trapping camp, he would know it, because they would not come past him.

If he positioned himself high in a lookout spot, he could command great stretches of country. Once he knew where they were bound, he could plan an ambush that they could not expect or resist.

Within two weeks he saw that they were heading up into the valleys leading to the crooked river. From his post high in a rocky cleft, he watched as they turned to follow the winding of the Snake. They would come beneath the shadow of the Ghost Mountains, and he had gone there as a youth with a band of hunters.

He could ambush them nicely, taking his revenge as well as their horses and the things they had traded for back at the rendezvous. He would return to his father loaded with plunder, leading a string of many animals, and then maybe the great man would approve of his son.

That had not happened since Lance was grown, and though he hated to think of it, he knew that most things he did were aimed at pleasing his father.

He overlooked the camp down on the blue lake, knowing that with three of them there it would be difficult to catch them unaware. Then he ran onto the track of a band of Shoshonni women and children, who seemed to be gleaning herbs and berries among the mountains.

He avoided them, for he had only a single purpose now. Lance hoped their warriors, wherever they hunted, would not spot his quarry, for that would spoil his own game.

He turned north, moving toward the Ghost Mountains over the roughest country he had ever tried to cross. There was a way down below, a long valley flanking a stream, but it was rich with game and plants, and he knew there was too much chance of finding others there. He wanted to leave no word of his passing among any tribes that might catch a glimpse of him.

At last he looked down on the river that wound like some wounded serpent among the ranges on its way to meet the Great River in the north that he had heard of in occasional encounters with Nez Percé from the lands beyond the mountains. No sign was there of any bands fishing or harvesting grass seeds or small birds. It was as if all those who lived in the mountains had gone far away after game he could not guess at.

As he moved northward Lance felt a vast calm settling over his heart. His mission was going to succeed; he had no doubt of that. This vacant stretch of land promised that. He was not surprised when he came up a terrible reach of rock and scrub and saw, beyond the height and across a green and narrow valley flanking the silver of the stream, the first of the pale mountains rising into the clouds.

No horse or man or child moved among the lush grasses. An elk grazed into view beyond a willow glade, and it was followed by several more. He found, once he made the terrible descent into the valley, the tracks of moose and bear and deer, beaver and skunk and wolf.

No man had set his moccasin here in a long while, for he could see that it had been days since the last rain. The cloud wrapping the heads of the mountains to the west promised that this might change soon, though Lance had found that rain came in the mountainous country far more often than in the plains beyond their wall.

He watered his horse, filled his waterskin, and moved rapidly upstream, passing those chilling heights that seemed to regard him without eyes for seeing, to be aware of him as if they were immense gods, sitting for a time on the earth and watching the small doings of men.

Kills with the Lance was not usually fanciful. He shook away the thought as he hurried up into the gentler slopes to the north, finding the trail that anyone traveling in this direction would naturally take if he intended to move into the mountains to the east.

Once he had scouted the country carefully, avoiding building fire or killing game for fear of warning anyone coming later that he had been here, he found a spot high on the side of a slope and made a camp there. His horse he pastured farther up, where a cup of grass was protected by a rim of rock grown with lodgepole pines and alders.

Then Kills with the Lance settled himself to wait. He might be impatient, as his father said, but he knew that in this one case he would wait until winter, if it took so long, for his prey to appear along the trail below him.

They would come. Every instinct he had told him that.

chapter

— 21 —

The Ghost Mountains were strange. Their pale peaks, rounding up into the sky, were troublesome to Second Son. It was as if there was an awareness in that rank of silvery shapes that made her feel as if someone watched over her shoulder.

Or was this feeling caused by something else? She shivered now, leading the way along the stream to the fork where a game trail came down from the forest to join the one marking the riverbank.

Billy Wolf, riding before her instead of in his cradle-board, gurgled softly, his small hands waving. There was a flick of motion ahead among the pines and firs, and three does and a fawn bounded away and disappeared among the thickets. Snip pricked his ears forward, but he didn't pursue the animals as he would have done a year ago.

"The small one has a good eye," she said over her shoulder.

Cleve, just behind with the lead rope for the string, chuckled. "Good ears, too. Good everything, come to think of it. We did a job making that one, Second Son. One day we'll have another, you think?"

She smiled silently. White men were not trained to control as her own kind had to be, and he had resisted her people's rule that years must separate children. To have too many small ones, unless you had a tribe for support, was dangerous. When Billy Wolf had four or five summers, then it would be time to think of another child.

Until then she would satisfy her husband as well as she could without taking the chance of becoming pregnant again. She had learned some things from a French-woman, wife of one of the traders at the rendezvous, that had relieved Yellow Hair of some of his frustration, and she was grateful for that.

Snip, who had been moving ahead just faster than Shadow's smooth walk, dropped back, his tongue lolling. The animal was becoming tired, she saw, and she pulled her mare to a halt. They had taught the dog to ride fairly patiently on one or the other of the pack-horses, and it was time for him to rest again.

She hated to think what it would be like without this tireless watchdog. Her son was safe when Snip stood guard. Besides which, she found she had grown fond of him as she had never done with another animal except Shadow. But death was a part of life, and she did not brood over it.

The sun was going down beyond the cloud-wrapped

peaks behind them as they went up into the forests beyond which the stark gray heights of the Absarokas thrust into the sky. It would be light for a while yet, and she did not pause except to rest the animals, forging along the slopes, edging upward as she watched for the trail leading over this series of ridges to the river that flowed between two ranges.

Cleve kicked Socks into a faster walk and came up beside her. "Do you feel funny?" he asked. He stared up and down, checking the sky and the game track they followed. "I have a feeling somebody's watching me."

"That is the mountains, I think," she said. Glimpses of those distant silver heads still peered at them, from time to time, between clumps of trees as they climbed. "But I do feel strange. I have not felt so since I was young and on the war trail with my father."

Snip wriggled, leaping down from the flat pack they had arranged for him to use when he rode. He growled deep in his throat, his hackles rising . . . and there came a yowl from the forest ahead. Lynx. Second Son laughed at her own alarm. Of course the dog would be wary of the big cat.

After that they traveled quietly, riding side by side when it was possible. She knew that Cleve, too, was feeling the nearness of the range that had become their home the past winter, and she was astonished at the warmth of her feeling. She was not used to considering a place as home—it was the tribe, the family together, that provided that security for her people.

When it grew dark, they stopped beneath an overhang of rock that thrust out from the slope above them, forming a natural shelter that would not only protect them from the light drizzle now falling but would also hide their fire. There was grass on the slope for the horses, and Cleve put them on long tethers so they would not stray while grazing.

Billy Wolf lay on his blanket before the newly kindled cone of fire with Snip beside him, muzzle on paws. Second Son glanced aside as she unrolled the bedding and cut meat from a haunch of the deer they had killed early that morning; she was feeling a growing unease. They had traveled too easily through country that she knew to be dangerous and filled with potential enemies.

Though she felt they must have put Kills with the Lance off their trail, something still troubled her mind. When Cleve returned, she patrolled the slopes about their camp thoroughly before returning, but she found no trace of any track but those of the beasts that belonged there.

Cleve had damped out the fire and wrapped Billy Wolf again in his swaddlings. Snip was lying just beneath the shelter of the rock, his eyes gleaming faintly in the light of the moon, which hung above the clouds, diffusing them to a dim glow above the overhanging trees.

"I'll watch. You sleep," Yellow Hair told her. "When I'm sleepy, I'll wake you. There's nothing to see anyway, except rain and tree trunks."

As if to deny his words, there came a long wail from high on the mountain above the camp. Cougar. She sat up suddenly, analyzing the sound she had heard.

Snip was already standing, his ears pricked forward, outlined against the wet gleam of the rock outside their shelter. Cleve put his hand on hers, and she felt the tension in his fingers.

"That came from a human throat," she said. She felt him nod agreement.

Without a word they bundled the few items they had used into a pack. Cleve crept out of the overhang silently, moving into the trees, and Second Son hauled the pack and the supplies left tied in bundles into the open and waited in the drizzle, with Billy Wolf on her back, while he brought the file of horses to meet her.

Without a word exchanged, they loaded the animals and led their mounts southward, along the easier slopes that would come at last to the stream some already called the Wind River. Second Son kept her ear cocked for any threatened snort or whiffle from the horses that might carry above the sound of the rain and betray them to the one who had uttered that cry from the heights.

It might be someone who didn't know they were on the mountain, though she could not believe that. Whoever had taken the trouble to climb so high up that forbidding angle had not done it on a whim. No, that cougar cry had been a promise of triumph. She felt that, when she remembered the sound. It had a gloating edge.

They came onto a broad, grassy flat near dawn, with the horses beginning to flag badly. Though the sky was gray, the rain had stopped sometime before. Snip had been riding for hours, and even she felt weary and chilled through.

They found a spot in a thicket for their camp, and Cleve loosed the horses in a nook cut back into the mountain behind, where they could rest and graze. They did not approach the river, which was here not much more than a deep creek, but watered the animals at a brook running down from the higher country. They build no fire but chewed jerky while Second Son nursed the infant.

The young fir and pine grew thickly, making good cover, and there they spent the day, watching by turns, sleeping, resting for the efforts of the night to come. When the sun began to sink behind the peaks to the west, Cleve put his head close to hers.

"I think Lance is waiting for us, somewhere along our way home. I think that was his voice we heard last night. Joe Ferris told us he was a smart fellow, and he warned us to

watch out for him. Just because Levreaux didn't see anybody watching our camp didn't mean there wasn't someone there. I believe that devil has been ahead of us all the
way."

Once the words were uttered, she knew that it had
been in her mind, too, since their parting with Ferris.
The Pawnee was an old enemy, and though she had
been lucky in her raids on his band, others had not.
More than one of the Tsistsistas had fallen in raids and
counterraids between their people.

"Then we must have eyes that see everything, ears that
hear all. We cannot risk him, for he took Snip. The next
time he might—"

"Take Billy Wolf," Yellow Hair finished for her. "I
been thinking of that for hours now. Anybody low enough
to steal your dog might just take your baby, too. But
what'd he do with him, if he did steal him?"

She laid her hands on her knees, regarding him soberly.
"He would rear him as a Pawnee, with his sons. He would
make our child into our enemy, an enemy of my people.
That would seem a fitting revenge to him, I think."

She heard Cleve's teeth grind together, and she felt
the same, though she did not show it. "We must go when
it becomes dark enough to hide us from above. We can
move through the trees. The mountain seems to slope
more easily beyond the next bend of the river, and there
we might try to go over the top, if the horses can
manage the climb."

"We'll find a way," he said. "I want to get on top of
that bastard and flush him out. I want to tackle him hand
to hand and wring his red neck!"

That was her precise feeling, but she said nothing.

They moved when it was dark, though the moon would
rise in a couple of hours. They must be well into the

trees, hidden from any watcher above them, when that happened. The horses stamped and snorted, but Cleve bound their jaws with looped thongs so they couldn't whinny. Then they set off, leading the animals as quickly as possible, higher and higher onto the slopes.

Above them the granite tops of the high Absarokas stabbed the sky with their angry peaks. Below, the valley opened out, without cover. Only in the mountains could they hope to escape their pursuer, and though the horses slipped and sweated and foamed around the loops, the two of them bullied the pack animals up the steeps.

Shadow moved quietly, easily, beside Socks. Her colt, half-grown now and almost as large as she, kept close to her side as if he felt the danger that threatened. Second Son, moving up and down the line of animals, touched her mare each time she passed her, taking comfort in the solid warmth of her sweaty hide.

By dawn they were over the first ridge. Ahead were steeper slopes, higher mountains that promised little comfort to anyone trying to cross them. Getting the horses over them was not going to be easy, if it was possible at all.

Once they were hidden in a steep-sided canyon where there was grass and water, she turned to Cleve. "We cannot force the horses to do this. We must hunt him, track him, kill him. I will not run before this warrior, for that is not my way."

Cleve stood solid and square against the clouded sky. His face was grim. "Yes. But what about the baby?"

"I will carry him on my back. I have had a dream, long ago, in which I faced great danger with a cradleboard tied to my shoulders. Though all seemed hopeless, I counted coup, and the dream ended. We cannot go on as we are doing. Let us hunt him down."

He stared up toward the high places, and she knew he was trying to sense a direction in which to search out their enemy. At that moment another shriek sounded, one that seemed so real she had to think for a moment to assure herself that it was human, not animal, as it echoed endlessly from the surrounding ridges and heights.

That one was what they had been waiting for. Second Son felt grim satisfaction well up in her as she stared toward the origin of the sound. He was behind them, still, high above the area they had crossed in the night.

"I'll climb," said Yellow Hair against her ear. "Carrying the baby will slow you down. You take a lower route. We'll see if we can't catch him between us. It's time we put an end to this bastard."

He looped his bow over his shoulder, his quiver of arrows attached. He put four knives about his person and shook his head regretfully as he discarded the Hawken that Bridwell had brought so far to him. She knew he was thinking of the rough country he must cross, going up and down like one of the horned ones in the mountains.

Second Son smiled as she secured her own weapons. Billy Wolf, tightly packed onto his cradleboard on her back, though he was getting too big for its confinement, was quiet.

Cleve bent and hugged the pair of them tightly for a moment. Then he set out up the nearest slope, and Snip, moving with an energy he hadn't shown in weeks, followed.

Second Son tried calling him back, but for once he did not obey. She could see that he was determined to go with Cleve, and at last she reconciled herself to that and set off along a lower route, making for a point below that from which the cry of the cougar had come.

Though she feared for her child, her heart beat with the joy of war. This was the thing she did best, and she could not regret it.

chapter
— 22 —

Cleve worried about Snip as he began climbing a rock face that would take him out of the canyon concealing the horses. The old dog wasn't able to go up a straight wall of stone, and there was no way he could help him, for it took everything he had to keep from falling off the cliff himself.

When he had a chance, he glanced back down to the dwindling patch of rubble from which he started. The third time, Snip was gone, and he sighed with relief. He had gone back to camp and would watch the horses. That was best.

His hands were cramping by the time he hauled himself onto the top of a rocky wall and lay flat, examining the country within his view. He checked the sun, which was now well above the ranges to the east, and pinpointed the area toward which he wanted to go. Luckily this was well to the north, and he could see no obvious difficulties like the wall he had just climbed.

He rose to a crouch and sped to a row of pine seedlings. They were spindly but green, at this elevation, despite the evidence all around that earlier generations had sprung up, lived for a time, and died. As he rolled into cover, something moved, and he tensed beneath a thick branch of needles, listening.

Snip slipped under the young trees and touched Cleve's face with a cold nose. How in hell had the dog managed to get here? There had to be an easier way than the one he'd taken, that was certain, and Snip had found it out. It wasn't the first time the dog had astonished his master.

He couldn't deny that he was glad to have the old fellow at his heels as he crept across open spots and sped through forested ones, keeping his goal before him as well as possible. This was going to be a hellacious job, and by the time he came to the place from which the cougar scream had come, it was likely that his quarry would have moved, on, searching for his prey. But there was nothing else to do, and he kept going, able to stay under cover by slipping down the slopes to the thicker forest.

He never caught any glimpse of Second Son, who had to be moving in the same direction on a lower level. He didn't expect to—she could disappear on an open plain, if she needed to do that. With tree and rock cover she moved like a ghost.

His impulse was to hurry. The sooner this danger was removed, the better he would feel, but he was too wise to risk it. This was rough country, and though he found no climbs as hard as the first had been, there were perilous places that taxed his strength and his balance.

Always he thought that Snip would be left behind, but every time he reached the end of a leap or a difficult scramble, he waited for a bit. Snip always arrived from an unexpected direction, panting and excited, and took up his position at Cleve's heels.

The morning wore on, and Cleve went more cautiously. His man was probably moving now, surveying the country, checking out any motion through the trees or between boulders. Cleve didn't want to confront him unexpectedly and trust to chance to survive the encounter. He wanted to trap the bastard and kill him quickly.

Noon found him moving along a spine of gray rock edged with a fringe of pine and fir. Big alders grew lower on the slope, providing good cover, and he made good speed as he ran toward a notch that promised another canyon at the end of the ridge. As he neared it Snip dashed past him and stopped, almost tripping him.

He trusted the old dog's senses far more than he did his own. Cleve dropped onto his belly and wriggled forward toward the notch. When he arrived, he risked only half an eye past the lip of stone as he surveyed the steep-sided cut below him.

It was empty. The bottom was so covered with weathered stone fallen from the sides that it couldn't possibly take the track of anyone passing that way. Snip bared his teeth when Cleve started to crawl over the edge and work his way down the rough rock of the wall. Not that way. His message was as clear as if it had been put into words.

Snip led the way to the right, along the edge of the rocky plateau. The ravine remained visible below, and as Cleve glanced down, very cautiously, he caught his breath. A scrap of feather, black and scarlet, glowed brightly in the sun streaming into the cut from directly overhead.

So tiny a thing should not have been visible at all, but against the gray-tan rock and in the full glare of sunlight, it was not to be missed.

As the warrior passed, Cleve saw, he had brushed his scalp lock against an overhanging spur, and it had rasped away a bit of the eagle feather in his hair. He never knew that the fluff fell soundlessly to the stony floor of the ravine, but it remained there to guide Cleve after its owner.

His heart was pumping steadily, his feet moving silently as he went, stooped and ready, a knife in his right hand and another ready to his left. Surely it would be soon now!

Again Snip stopped him, and ahead he found that the cut disappeared into the mountain. A tunnel, dug by some long-ago stream perhaps, seemed to run far back into the stone. But still Snip warned him not to go down.

Why had Lance gone back into that cave? He was from the plains and couldn't possibly know if it emerged someplace that would put him nearer his goal. Or— Cleve chilled at the thought—was he luring some pursuer into a trap? Only Second Son could be the one he might think to trick so. He had to get down!

But Snip bared his teeth again when he leaned over to survey the descent. Then he turned and ran uphill, his tail wagging imperatively.

For a moment Cleve was torn between concern for his wife and trust in his dog. But he knew that Second Son was a match for any warrior, and she would not be caught unaware, no matter what the trap. And Snip had proved himself a thousand times during their long years together.

He set out at a lope, following the skinny tail that flicked in and out of tree shadow as the animal headed for some unknown goal. In a half hour he came through a tangle of chokecherry and bramble to find Snip waiting for him.

His tongue hanging nonchalantly from the corner of his mouth, the dog sat beside a hole that was almost like a rough well. When Cleve knelt and peered downward, he could see nothing but darkness. It looked like a perfect spot to find rattlesnakes.

Without waiting for him to make up his mind, Snip leaped into the hole. Cleve gasped and bent far over. Below, some dozen feet beneath the surface, he saw something moving. White and black—Snip had found bottom and was waiting for him.

The dry rustle of rattles did nothing to encourage Cleve to join his dog, but he gritted his teeth, swished a broken branch furiously around inside the opening, and then dangled his feet into the hole, feeling for something on which to set his toe.

Tree roots helped. When they ran out, he was within a few feet of the bottom, and he loosed his toehold and dropped. The tiny bit of sky above only made the darkness all around him seem worse. He could hear quiet slithers, too, and that did nothing to calm him.

There was a tangle of dead roots there, with leaves that had fallen through the hole, and he knelt, took out his flint and steel, and struck spark after spark. After what seemed hours a curl of smoke rose from the crumbled leaves he had prepared and a wisp of flame came to life.

It was no task to make a torch, though the dry stuff would not burn for long. He took several lengths of the spongy root for spares and started off after Snip along a round tunnel that still showed the marks where water had flowed beneath the earth.

The dirt beneath his moccasins was smooth, cold, slick

with moisture. His steps made no sound, and he concentrated on looking ahead.

From a distance he heard someone move, the sound strangely distorted by its travel up the winding tube. If this was Lance, Cleve was almost there; he dashed out the torch to keep from alerting his enemy and crept along after Snip, whose hard tail kept wagging against his knees, keeping him in the right path.

They emerged onto a shelf of rock beneath a crack in the stone above them. A thin beam of gray light shot down into the lower area. There Cleve saw Kills with the Lance, his bow drawn, his gaze fixed on something lost in the shadows ahead of him.

Cleve peered into the murk to see Second Son step forward, her knife in her hand, their son's cradleboard showing beyond her shoulder.

"You have come after us," she said. Again she moved forward. "And now I come after you, Pawnee. I have stolen horses, I have stolen lives, and now I steal you from your people."

Her words were brave, but the arrow aimed at her heart could cross the distance between them before she could possibly throw the knife. Lance stepped forward, his shoulders set.

Cleve dived off the shelf on which he stood and hit the warrior high on his shoulders, sending him onto his face among the rubble of the cave's floor. But Lance was strong and wily, and with a wriggle he freed himself and rolled upright again, his bow lost but his knife appearing in his hand—one of the good trade knives Ashworth had brought to the rendezvous.

Cleve stepped aside as the man lunged, but Lance ducked aside and caught him in the belly with a shoulder. For the first time in a very long while, the trapper found himself matched by an opponent. The knife hand went up and Cleve set his heels against the rock and tried to roll.

A bolt of black and white shot over him and hit the big Indian with a thump. Snip was snarling like a mad dog, his lips curled back, his canines dripping saliva, his ruff erect about his flattened ears. Never had Cleve seen his dog so furious.

Lance gave a terrible cry and grappled with the animal. Before Cleve could get to his feet and recover his own knife, Second Son ran forward, ready to stab him, but man and dog rolled so desperately that there was no way to keep from cutting Snip. Cleve stepped beside her, weapon ready for an opportunity for use, and they watched in amazement.

Lance's hand managed to clear his knife. Snip, his head buried in the man's neck, was covered in blood even before the blade came out and struck into his side, despite Cleve's desperate kick that sent the knife sailing to clank against the rock of the wall.

Then Lance went limp, his hand dropping beside him in the faint beam of light. Blood was bright on his fingers, and when Cleve lifted Snip off the dead man, the dog's coat was streaked with red.

But Snip wasn't dead. Not yet. The brown eyes opened, and the skinny tail gave the faintest of wags.

Second Son made a sound—not a sob, for she was Tsistsistas—and loosed the cradleboard, freeing Billy Wolf from confinement. She held the baby close to the rough fur of Snip's face, and the dog tried to lick the round nose so near his own.

Billy Wolf made a small crow of greeting, but it was too late. The eyes glazed, the tail fell limp, and Snip was no longer confined inside the worn body in Cleve's arms.

Cleve felt tears rise behind his eyes, but he was a grown man, a trapper, a coureur de bois. Such men didn't weep over their dogs, no matter how great the loss might be.

Instead he looked down into the half-open eyes of the Pawnee. The face was not an evil one, despite its oiled scalp and defiant roach of stiff hair. This man had a family, too. Cleve wondered what compulsion had made him give up everything for the possibility of vengeance, but the stiff form offered no explanation, and he turned away from it without even straightening the limbs.

Second Son held Billy Wolf close and turned down the long dark passage up which she had come through blackness. "If you had not come, he might have killed us," she said. "I should not have gone into that dark way, for the dream warned me many moons ago. And yet I could not stop. I was compelled to follow him. Why do you think that might be?"

"I've given up on dreams," Cleve said, reaching to touch his son with his free hand. "I've had some that turned me cold and afraid, but I've about decided that you can't get around what's going to happen, no matter how you try. You just keep plugging along, and somehow it'll come out all right."

After a long while they came out into the shady afternoon. The sky, now clear of clouds, was lit with sun, but the ravine was dark.

"I want to bury him," said Cleve. "I don't care about Kills with the Lance. He's got a grave a king would envy. But I don't want Snip eaten by scavengers."

"There is a place." She pointed up the ravine. "A stone fell out and left a deep hole. It would make a good grave for him. I will show you."

It did, indeed, make a good grave. The hole was big enough for a horse, in fact, and there was a rock, large enough to seal it, that was almost loose enough to sink into the space on its own. When Snip had been laid inside, Cleve pried away the edges holding the top boulder, which rumbled down to hide the hole entirely.

Harking back to his days when he was learning Latin from his mother, Cleve took his oldest knife and began scratching a painful inscription into the rock:

CAVE CANEM

"What do you say with your sign?" asked his wife. She came close with Billy Wolf, peering at the letters.

"Beware of the dog," Cleve answered, his tone gruff.

Then they turned back toward the valley and the easier way to their camp. Even in darkness, which was coming quickly now, they would find it, though there would be no yip of welcome.

But they were near their own Shadow Mountains, their hidden place that would keep their son safe for a time yet. The coming winter would be busy, and by next year Billy Wolf would be walking and even talking.

"In a couple of years," Cleve said as they trudged along, "let's go back and visit your family. Then"—he glanced through the dimness at her face—"maybe I could take you and the boy here back to see my own folks. Somehow I'm not scared of Pa anymore. I can face him now."

She smiled sideways at him. "That is good. But I think I might stay with my people and let you take our son to your people without me. I have seen the white men. I have listened to their words. It would be best, I think, to remain in my own place."

They came near the camp, but only muffled snorts and hoof thumps from the horses could be heard. Cleve heaved a sigh. The immediate danger was over. Lance was gone, and his people would never know what happened to him, though old Buffalo Grass, if Emile Prevot was right about him, might guess pretty accurately.

If they were lucky, there would be no major problem now, before they came to their Shadow Mountain valley. And if they were unlucky—Cleve grinned as he stretched out his legs to the fire Second Son had kindled. If they were unlucky, God help anyone who came up against the two of them.

AFTERWORD

The first great rendezvous for trappers was organized and held by William H. Ashley in the summer of 1825. The location was a basin at the junction of the stream some called the Sketskedee, now called Green River, and the creek that ran down from the adjacent mountains to meet the larger stream.

I have based the rendezvous in this book closely upon that original one, though I have, of course, added elements, particularly the rules governing conduct there, for my own literary purposes. I have also changed names and added fictional characters to that event.

After sending his bands of trappers into the mountains, Ashley returned to St. Louis, Missouri, to establish himself in politics, but the apparent failure of his trapping enterprise, for which he had borrowed heavily, almost bankrupted him. However, at the last moment a letter from Jedediah Smith, the famous trapper and mountain man and later his partner in the Rocky Mountain Fur Company, arrived just in time to reassure Ashley's creditors and allow him to stock his expedition to the trapping country for the purchase of the furs Smith described in his letter.

Though Ashley had expected only his own people, in the main, to attend this rendezvous, he found to his surprise that others, from the long-established French coureurs de bois to some of those American and British trappers who had been trading with the Hudson's Bay Company, arrived ready for bargaining. There were also Indians from several tribes wanting to take advantage of the opportunity.

I have made some changes in a number of historical matters, but in one thing I was deliberately accurate. This first rendezvous was not the orgy of sex and whiskey that later ones became, principally because nobody had anticipated the market for women that would automatically come into being. So the Henry's Fork get-together was relatively staid, by contrast with later ones, although there must have been a lot of drinking (though the whiskey was well watered) as well as a bit of hanky-panky, given the presence of so many sex-starved trappers.

As might be expected, the markup on trade goods was large—anything from fifty to four hundred percent is the estimate given in *William H. Ashley*, by Richard M. Clokey (University of Oklahoma Press, c. 1980). This, added to the profit on the furs for which the goods were traded, formed the basis for his financial recuperation and later political career.

After seeing how profitable the venture was going to

be, his partner, Jedediah Smith, and others bought out his interest in 1826 and Ashley returned to Missouri for a life in part as business representative for the Rocky Mountain Fur Company. Eventually he became a Congressman from his state.

Those trappers on the payroll of the fur company were paid two dollars a pound for their catch, as opposed to the three dollars a pound paid to those trapping independently. The cost of trade goods meant that though they were credited with a lot of money as they sold their plews, unless they were inhumanly conservative they left with not much more cash than they brought.

It is estimated that of any hundred men going out to trap in the Rockies, only about sixteen of them remained alive after two years. That, to some extent, gives an idea of the dangers found in this wild land by everyone, red or white, as they eked out an existence.

Some have suggested that it was the contact with Native Americans that kindled the original notion of personal freedom in those expatriate Europeans. Given the lack of any such idea in the Old World, that seems quite possible, for each Indian in most tribes, except for some of the more southern or Aztecan ones, was his own master. Chiefs were planners, not bosses, and there was no penalty for telling them, "No, I won't go to war today. I want to go hunting instead."

This was the pattern, conscious or not, that probably worked its way into the subconscious of those forging westward, meeting and interacting with the tribes. In light of our treatment of those people, later, we proved to be ungrateful for the concept of freedom they may have given our ancestors.

If you enjoyed **WILDERNESS RENDEZVOUS**
by John Killdeer, be sure to look
for the next novel in his
MOUNTAIN MAJESTY series:

B L O O D   K I N

Mountain man, Cleve Bennett, and his six-year-old
son, Billy Wolf, set out on a journey from the rugged
frontier that is their home, eventually tracing the Little
Sac back to Cleve's family homestead in Missouri.
Cleve's father, mellowed with age and disability,
welcomes his son, but Mattie Bennett is displeased to
find that Cleve has married a Cheyenne woman and is
raising a "savage" son. But when a dangerous neighboring clan, the Tollivers, decide to make trouble for
the Indian boy, the Bennetts must band together to
protect their Blood Kin. . . .

Look for Mountain Majesty Book 4: **BLOOD KIN**,
on sale in February 1993,
wherever Bantam Domain Books are sold.